Hard to Get

(Book One of the Hard to Get Series)

by Jenny Gardiner

www.jennygardiner.net

What people are saying about Jenny Gardiner's books:

Red Hot Romeo

"Awesome". So enjoyed the romantic chemistry between the two characters. Read it non stop into the wee hours. Highly recommend this book

-- Mrs. K

Blue-Blooded Romeo

"Another brilliant, fun read from Jenny Gardiner. The book is fun to read and I thoroughly enjoyed every word. Jenny Gardiner has put the fun back into romance books and I look forward to each book in this delightful series."

-- Anne Blyth

"I had planned on only reading a few chapters at first but couldn't put it down. A terrific storyline, well-developed and extremely relatable characters, what's not to love?? Great read!"

-- Samantha Reeves

Big O Romeo

"I could not put this book down. Warning don't start this book late at night as you will not want to stop reading.

-- Di

Chapter One

LOLA Quigley's hands trembled against her keyboard as she opened the email from the Food Channel, something she'd been waiting months for. Before she clicked on it, she closed her eyes and sat back in the chair. Running her fingers through her long brown hair, she took a deep, cleansing breath. If the response was negative, then oh well. She'd move on, and things would somehow work out. She reminded herself she needed to be at peace with whatever happened since it was all out of her control anyhow. Besides, after all she'd been through over the past handful of years, she'd find another way. Lola was resilient and she'd figure it out. She always did.

As she squinted her hazel eyes, her pointer finger hovered over her inbox before she clicked on the email and opened it up.

"It's only an email," she whispered like a mantra. "It's only an email." And then she drummed up the courage to read the damned thing.

Dear Miss Quigley,

Congratulations! You've been chosen to compete in an upcoming episode of Shop till you Drop*! Our producers loved your demo submission—especially when your cat jumped up on the table when you were eating your finished meal, which they thought was a charming touch. We loved when she started licking that corn smut and prickly pear soup you'd made—very*

creative side dish, by the way. And clearly delicious enough for a picky cat to enjoy. Please contact me at your earliest convenience and I'll provide details. We're excited to have you on the show!
Best,
Amy Ming, Producer

Lola sat for a moment, staring in disbelief. She had been selected as a competitor on one of the most popular cooking shows in the country, where cooks raced the clock and each other to shop for and create a prizewinning meal using selected nonperishable, donated items cast off from food banks.

The tall, athletic brunette knew she had her work cut out for her, but she'd been preparing for this for years, like it or not. Plenty of times since things went so wrong, back when that jerk Levi did what he did, she'd gotten by on the kindness of food bank and church food pantry donations. And yeah, a lot of times what was donated were ingredients that perhaps seemed aspirational when the donor purchased them. She was good at making something from nothing. Like when she found in her donation bag a box of make-it-yourself German spaetzle, red curry paste, fish oil, a bag of pork rinds, and a jar of deviled eggs. She'd turned it into a makeshift German-Thai dish, a sort of carbonara that didn't taste half bad after she'd worked her magic.

Now that she'd pulled herself from the pit of despair, where she'd languished for far too long, and could splurge on a half-decent meal out once in a while, she would test that rumbling-belly-what-am-I-gonna-eat muscle memory to win the $100,000 prize. Winning that money would give her the chance to pay it forward by launching a mobile soup kitchen to feed those in the community who struggled to feed themselves.

Having made it this far, she *had* to win. Whatever it took, she'd do it. She'd make darn good and sure that the legacy of Levi leaving her at the altar would be one of vindication. After "the wedding that wasn't," she'd been so distraught she dropped out of school and failed at a succession of low-paying jobs for years. Yet this phoenix's rise from the ashes would be one for the ages because she intended to win *Shop till You Drop* come hell or high water.

Chapter Two

SOMETIMES Levi Patton indulged his less noble side, wondering what he'd done to deserve seeing his life's work swirling down the crapper in one epic flush.

Because boy, had his career done a sudden one-eighty, from meteoric success as the boy genius on the DC food scene to the culinary equivalent of a fifteen-car pileup on the interstate. It all started after the vaunted food critic for the *Washington Chronicle* encountered an unmistakable piece of a rat's tail floating in his bouillabaisse.

Holy crap, was that a bad day in his life. He'd suspected the man seated at the table by the window was the much-anticipated undercover food critic and had alerted his staff to ensure the man's meal was perfect. He oversaw each dish as it left the kitchen. That's why he knew a rat appendage hadn't found its way into his fine French fusion cuisine under his watchful eye. Someone had sabotaged him, and he had a good idea who it was but had never been able to prove it.

Rumor had it the critic at first thought it was an antenna that had fallen into the broth from the langoustine lobster Levi used in it. But upon further inspection, there was no doubt that it was, indeed, a rodent tail, complete with a core layer of bone covered by that telltale hairless, circular-ridged skin. Whoever had it out for Levi knew what he was doing, no question about that.

His demise was fast and painful. In a flash, he lost a restaurant he'd worked years to open only months earlier to rave reviews. But worse still, he lost his reputation and was now known as Rat-Boy, the moniker the tabloids found it cute to give him.

Levi pressed the heels of his hands to his brown eyes, trying to knead the stress of his life away to no avail. He sat down at the makeshift desk he'd set up in the living room of the almost-empty efficiency apartment he'd recently moved into to save money and switched on his computer. He then tried to massage his weary scalp by pressing his fingers through his wavy brown hair, but even that didn't help. It seemed the headache that overtook him months ago had parked itself inside his brain and wasn't planning to depart anytime soon.

What had he done to deserve this? Well, at least this in particular? Nothing, really. Had he made some poor decisions in his life, maybe some that led to hurting people who didn't deserve it? Yep. No doubt about it. In fact, there were likely people who thought he was the worst person to walk the face of the earth. Like, say, Lola Quigley, his high school sweetheart who he'd planned to meet at the justice of the peace to get married way back when they were young and stupid. The very Lola he blew off, for reasons not even worth mulling over.

And while yeah, that was about the shittiest thing he could have done, he was a kid back then, and he screwed up. He'd sent about a bazillion letters (not to mention emails and text messages) of apology—since all of his calls went unanswered. At some point, he stopped trying to persuade Lola that he wasn't a flaming asshole. Because even he knew that deep down, he had to have been one to have committed such a hurtful act. Even if it was at her mother's behest, which was why he did it, it cost Lola dearly, emotionally, and no doubt took a toll on her self-esteem.

Levi rubbed his eyes again. If he had a dollar for every time he'd gone over this in his brain… Yet a whole lotta good it would do him. He scrolled through his emails, seeing if he had gotten any responses to the many job applications he'd submitted. Nothing popped out at him until he saw something that said it was from the Food Channel. No doubt some investigative reporter wanting to humiliate him even more.

Instead, he found an email from a producer, the contents of which were rather curious.

Greetings—
I am the producer of the popular Shop till you Drop *show in which cooks compete for prize money by making meals with some of the unusual foods donated to food banks. Normally we pit less-seasoned cooks against one another, but in light of your unfortunate circumstances, we thought it might be interesting to give you a chance to demonstrate your culinary skills against some top-tier home cooks and rising professionals and see what might unfold. I hope you'll consider this opportunity to join us in this adventure. I think it could go a long way toward rehabilitating your faltering career and giving America the chance to forgive you. I look forward to your reply.*
Best,
Amy Ming, Producer

Amy Ming. Why did that name ring a bell? Amy Ming. Ming. Ming. Ming. He held up his finger. She'd been a newly hired line cook at his restaurant, hadn't she? It was like her third week on the job when it all went to crap. Why on earth would she want anything to do with him? Was she going to try to shame him on national television?

He shook his head. *Nah.* She seemed like too nice of a woman to do that. Weird she'd reach out to him like this, but maybe she had her reasons. Maybe she could help him solve the mystery of what happened that night. What could it hurt for him to go on the show? It was impossible to embarrass himself even further—there was no place to go but up. And it wasn't like he'd have an issue with the competition. Sure, maybe they'd want to outdo him. Maybe he'd go easy on them, at least at first. With any luck, even if they did recognize him as the Rat-Boy, they'd take a little pity on him, cut him some slack, and give him a tiny chance for redemption.

It was a long shot, for sure. But what he needed was a Hail Mary pass right now. Like it or not, he'd stand tall, cook his ass off, and win the prize, enough to at least dig himself out of the financial hole he'd found himself in.

Okay, Amy Ming, Producer. You're on. Bring it, baby.

Chapter Three

LOLA pulled the tray of crispy curried chickpeas with rosemary from the oven, kicking the oven door shut with her heel. She used her favorite fish spatula to transfer the chickpeas onto a paper towel to cool off, popping one into her mouth to sample.

"Oh God, so delicious," she said, breathing out hard, fanning her hand near her open mouth. As if that would keep the chickpea from frying her tongue. "Jesus, that was hot. Whitney, you've gotta try one."

She placed two of the round balls on the spatula and offered a taste to her best friend, Whitney Brookings.

She blew on them to cool them off, then popped a couple into her mouth. Her blue eyes widened. "Whoa, that's amazingly delish," she said, reaching for a few more before Lola swatted her away with the spatula.

"Sorry. I need them for my practice dish," she said. "You can have some more once I finish this."

"Whatcha making?"

Lola scrunched up her nose. "Well, I'm trying to throw together weird things and hoping for the best. That's how this competition goes. I picked up a couple of containers of Vienna sausages—"

"Those are nasty."

"Tell me about it," Lola said. "Anyhow, I've gotta use two weird things like this that people unload when they donate food. So, I thought about maybe a simple Vienna sausage in a saffron cream sauce with the roasted curried chickpeas. That way I can play around and see how it tastes."

Whitney shrugged. "Might as well. I mean, not like I'm planning to eat here tonight." She winked. "The judges have no choice but to try it." She stuck her finger down her throat and pretended to gag.

"Dude, this is the kind of stuff I used to eat on a regular basis. I'd make a great judge on this show!"

"I'm sorry, Lol," her friend said. "That rotten Levi sure did you no favors."

"Trust me, I've spent far too much time badmouthing Levi Patton, but maybe in this case it all did work out for the best. Had I not drowned in the pit of despair like I did, I'd never have learned to cook crap with panache and land on *Shop till you Drop!*"

"Okay, so we're done bashing Levi?" Whitney squinted at Lola, who shook her head.

"Oh, hell no, honey." She laughed out loud. "We made a veritable Olympic sport of badmouthing Levi—no point in stopping now."

Whitney dragged her hand across her brow in relief. "Thank goodness. I don't know what I'd have done if I had to stop that. Too much dead airtime to fill otherwise."

"Not gonna lie," Lola said as she deglazed the pan with an Austrian Riesling. "You'd probably be able to start a part-time job. Or take up a hobby."

They both laughed. "Do you still have that Levi Patton voodoo doll I bought you back in college?"

Lola poured heavy cream into the pan and stirred, scraping up the pan drippings, then tossed a generous pinch of saffron and salt in and some freshly ground pepper. She grabbed a spoon from the utensil drawer and took a taste, shaking her head.

"Not bad," she said. "You want a taste?"

Whitney held her hands up. "I'll take a hard pass. Canned premade, unidentified meat products are where I draw the line."

"Your loss."

"I'll suffer the consequences."

"Ahhh. Sorry I got distracted and forgot about the voodoo doll. Yeah, it's somewhere." She nodded toward the other end of the kitchen. "It used to be in that drawer that has all the stupid things you don't know what to do with. Like random screws, plug adaptors, rubber bands, twist ties, and stray paper clips."

"So you knew exactly where it was without even thinking twice?"

Lola threw her a side-eye. "No. Well, maybe. But only because it was always handy to keep it in the kitchen."

"Because?"

Lola rolled her eyes. "Duh." She held up her chef's knife.

"Don't wield that thing at me." Whitney pretended to protect her face with her hands.

"Silly! I meant I used to stick the knife into the heart of the Levi doll. It was my little passive-aggressive stress relief."

"Ha! I'd say that was straight-up aggressive. No passive whatsoever."

"Whatever. But I haven't used it in a while. I'm so over Levi Patton. Sure, he was a supreme asshole for ditching me the way he did. But that was a lifetime ago. And maybe I owe him a little acknowledgment. After all, I learned to overcome adversity thanks to him."

"Adversity-smershity. I'd rather you'd learned about tender loving-kindness from him instead. You know how many shirts got stained with mascara from your tears back then?"

"I'm sorry about that. I did switch to waterproof after a while. But look at it this way: I learned about tender lovingkindness from people like you. So it's all good."

"Awww, that's why you're my BFF, Lola Q."

"And why I love you to the moon and back, my friend."

"So, you ready for this crazy thing you're about to do?"

"As ready as I'll ever be." Lola wiped a bead of sweat from her brow. "It's gonna be weird. I've never cooked competitively before. I think the others might be hard-core professionals who've done this repeatedly. But what I lack in experience, I have in desire. I want to win this thing and I'll do my damnedest to succeed."

"You've got a lot of people rooting for you."

"Wish you could come with me. I sure could use the moral support."

"You'll be fine," Whitney said, reaching for a spoon. "I know I said I didn't want to try this, but it smells too darned good." She scooped up a spoonful and slipped it into her mouth. "Holy mother of God, Q. This is insane. You are so gonna win this thing."

"As long as they don't pit me against like some Michelin-starred chef, I know I've got it in the bag."

"Fuck any Michelin-starred anything. You're Lola Quigley and you're going to kick some Michelin-starred ass, baby. I can feel it in my bones."

Chapter Four

LEVI squeezed the jalapeno and chive aioli sauce from a squirt bottle onto three dinner plates, artfully smudging the tail of each squirt, then dabbing confetti dots of cream around the edge of the plate. He scooped a serving of Mexican corn salad in the center and delicately set three scallops atop the salad, then crumbled cotija cheese and drizzled lime juice from his hand. He cleaned up a few wayward smudges of food from the edges of the plates and wiped his hands with the dishtowel draped from his apron.

"*Buen provecho*," he said in Spanish in honor of his Mexican-inspired meal as he delivered the plates to the dining room, where his sister and her husband were almost licking their chops awaiting their meal.

"Have I told you what a treat it is to have a world-famous chef as a brother?" his sister Jules said, elbowing her husband Domenico as she grabbed her knife and fork and dug into her meal. "Am I right?" Her husband nodded in agreement.

But her brother grimaced as he sat down next to Jules. "More like infamous," he said, curling his lip.

Jules set her fork down and wagged her finger. "I thought we've been over this about a thousand times," she said. "What happened was wrong and you know and I know and we all know that something fishy happened. I swear we'll get to the bottom of it. And it does not diminish that you are the most a-fucking-mazing cook I've ever had the pleasure of being related to." She gave him a big smile for emphasis.

Levi heaved a sigh. "Honestly if I didn't love cooking so much I'd walk away from everything at this point."

"And do what?" His sister rolled her eyes. "You were always only going to be a chef and you know it!"

He shook his head. "I dunno. A welder, maybe."

She laughed. "A welder? That's a weird one. What the hell made you come up with that?"

He shrugged. "I figure I'm good with my hands. And you probably need to have good steady hands for that job."

"Steady hands?" Domenico said. "Maybe you should be a dentist."

Jules spread her fingers wide and splayed her hand across her husband's face. "Ignore him. He can't think and eat at the same time."

He held up his hands in surrender. "I'm only trying to help. But I'll be happy to eat more." He redirected his attention to his food.

"Thanks, Dom, but I don't think at this late date in my life I should consider dental school. I'd be geriatric by the time I finished all that training."

"Not like you're old, Levi." His sister knit her brow. "You're like a year younger than I am."

"And you're fifty-two."

She pretended to slap him. "I am not! I'm still a half a year away from thirty. Don't age me needlessly."

Domenico stood up and walked toward the kitchen with his plate. "This is freaking awesome, brother."

"You ought to make this for that show thingy." His sister pointed at the plate for emphasis.

Levi laughed. "If only," he said. "It doesn't work like that, unfortunately."

Hard to Get

"What do you mean?"

"It's a competition and they give you weird shit to put together to make a meal."

"Like what kind of weird shit?"

He shook his head. "I'm not sure. To be honest, I haven't done any research."

"How the hell do you expect to win if you haven't even studied up on it?"

Levi rolled his eyes. "Come off it. It's a couple of lame chefs who probably don't even have knife skills, and the host tells you to do something with pickled pig's feet, demiglace, and a jar of maraschino cherries. At least I'll have a better idea about what to do than they will."

"I hope you know what you're talking about, baby brother. You need this to go well, so maybe you can get back into the game."

"What if I don't want to get back into the game?"

"Well, you're sure not suited to being a welder. Plus, you spent your meager inheritance on culinary school. You'd better milk that cow dry."

He ran his fingers through his hair. "I don't know what I want, Jules. Maybe I want to go back when life was simpler."

"You mean like when you were going to meet Lola at the courthouse and get married even though you were so young you couldn't even grow a proper beard?" She shook her head. "I mean, we loved Lola, but seriously, dude. Imagine if you had gotten married before you were even twenty years old! That would have been nuts!"

He stared at his plate for a moment, pushing kernels of corn with his fork. "I dunno. Maybe it would have been much better. We could have been happy together. Life would have been easier."

"You're deluding yourself if you think marrying young like that would have made things simpler. You'd have been poor and hungry and working your ass off."

"Yeah, so now I'm poor and hungry and not working my ass off."

She tipped her head. "Okay, fine. You've got a point there. But you weren't poor—you were making gobs of money. Before the whole, uh, thing. And this"—she stretched her arms out—"this is temporary. Come off it, Levi. You're practically a Michelin-starred chef. You were pegged as the 'boy genius' of the DC culinary scene. You need to be vindicated, that's all. And this *Shop till you Drop* show is going to redeem you. Mark my words."

Her husband lifted his head for the first time from his meal. "I remember Lola." He looked lost in wistful thought. "She was the one with those great biceps, right?" Jules elbowed him in the side and he swatted her away. "We liked Lola. You ever talk to her?"

Levi pursed his lips. "Not even once since I no-showed."

"You gotta admit, that was kind of a dick move to not show up," Domenico said.

Levi furrowed his brow. "It's not like I didn't try to get ahold of her. I called. I texted. I called some more. I even wrote a letter. She ghosted me."

"Can't say I blame her," his brother-in-law said, holding out his plate for seconds.

"What, you talk smack at me and then you want me to feed you more?"

"At least you're a quick read." Domenico fist-bumped his brother-in-law. "You know I can only give you shit since we're good friends."

"Yeah, I get it."

Hard to Get

"You ever think about her?" His sister lifted a brow.

"I was too busy to look back for a long time," he said, handing Domenico his refilled plate. "But I've had too much time on my hands, and I'd be lying if I said she hasn't crossed my mind."

"You should try to track her down. You could use some female company."

Levi laughed. "You have got to be kidding me. If she ever saw me again, she might chop off my dick with a rusty butter knife." He winced as he thought about that. "Trust me, I don't need female companionship that much."

"You'd better start looking for someone somewhere or I'm going to bring home people from work."

"You work with mice. In a lab."

"Sometimes there are people in there too."

He shook his head. "Thanks, I think I've got this under control. Now if you'll excuse me, I've got an early flight to catch in the morning."

Jules stood up and gave her brother a big hug. "You can do this. Go there and kick some ass and take names."

Levi wasn't sure he even wanted to find out the names of his fellow competitors, all of whom knew he'd be the one wearing the bullseye. And he was more than certain he was dreading this competition more than he cared to admit.

Chapter Five

LOLA wheeled her carry-on up to the check-in kiosk at Washington Dulles Airport. She'd given herself plenty of time to get through check-in and security; she didn't want anything to get in the way of her and the $100,000 prize that loomed before her like a mirage in the desert.

As she hoisted her bag onto the security conveyor belt, she heard a man several rows over in another line raising his voice.

"What do you mean, I can't take my knives on the flight?" he said, his voice combative.

"I'm sorry, sir, but all knives must be checked through to their final destination," the security guard said.

"But I'm a professional chef. These are valuable—they're my prized possessions. I can't risk them being stolen from my suitcase!" He pounded his fist on the edge of the belt, and two guards escorted him away from the other passengers toward a nearby room. Lola couldn't quite make out the guy's face—the best she could get was a partial profile view. She couldn't imagine why he thought he could bring knives into the cabin of a plane.

Shrugging, she shook her head. "Moron," she muttered.

Once she navigated what seemed like the three miles of walking to her gate, she zoomed to an airport convenience store and picked up a bottle of water, a bag of barbecue chips, a bag of Sour Patch Kids, and the latest issue of *People* magazine, then grabbed an espresso, a muffin, an apple, and a banana. She loved her some good gossip rags on a flight and needed a stash of boredom food for the trip too. Once seated at the gate, she watched planes taxiing on the runway outside the windowed walls of the airport in the still-dark sky. These early flights were the worst. She already felt like she'd pulled an all-nighter to get to this point and still had most of the day on an airplane to get through. Maybe she'd luck out and have an empty seat next to her. She could contort her body into something that resembled a sleeping position for an hour or two of shut-eye.

Finally, the gate crew announced they'd begin preboarding, so she moved into her assigned cattle-herding line for the process. Which was when she heard that loud voice again.

"What do you mean, I can't upgrade to first class?" The same man with the knives was standing at the counter nearby, arguing with a gate agent. That dude was having a shit day.

"But I was told I could upgrade when I got to the gate," he said, pounding a fist yet again, this time on the counter.

"I'm sorry, sir, but those seats are all filled. If you'd been here twenty minutes ago, you might have gotten one." She handed him back his boarding pass.

"Well, what about business class at least?"

She shook her head as she stared at the screen. "Ahhh, bad news: looks like the aisle seat you were assigned was taken. The only thing I've got left is this center seat."

"What?" The man's voice went up a full octave. She hoped they didn't seat him anywhere near her for this flight. It would be worse than sitting next to a crying baby.

"I'm sorry, sir, but please, if you could get in line to board, we're trying to get this flight out on time this morning."

Lola was dying to get a good look at the jerk who was causing such a commotion, but her line was moving forward. She pulled out her phone to open her airline app so the nearby agent could scan her boarding pass, then made her way down the jet bridge and onto the plane.

Once settled into her seat, she kept her fingers crossed, hoping she could spread out with the empty seat in the middle.

A flight attendant announced on the PA system that they had a few more passengers waiting to board and then they'd prepare for takeoff. Yes! She did a mental high-five. Surely, that extra twelve or so inches of seating would be all hers!

But then she heard that gruff but familiar voice, though she couldn't make out the words he was uttering.

She squinted as she looked up. The glare of the overhead lights kept her from seeing his face properly. "What did you say?"

"I need to get to my seat."

She thrust out her lower lip in disappointment. So close, yet so far.

A flight attendant walked by, checking that all luggage compartment doors were closed tightly. "Sir, please get to your seat and secure your seatbelt so we can prepare for takeoff."

He glared at her. "I still need to put my bag up here."

"I'm sorry, but there's no room. This flight is full. I'll have to gate check your bag and you can get it upon arrival in Los Angeles."

"Are you joking?"

"Sorry, no more room on the plane." The flight attendant held up her hands, palms up.

Hard to Get

"First off, I was late getting to the plane because stupid security wouldn't let me bring my knives on board. I had to go pay for a whole other piece of luggage so I'd be allowed to bring these with me. Then I had to race through security again, and once at the gate, I tried to upgrade my seat—as I was told I'd be able to do when I checked in originally—but learned not only could I not upgrade, even to what, peasant class? Do you have peasant class? Because I couldn't even get that. They gave my aisle seat away to some other undeserving passenger, and now they've relegated me to the cockroach seat, which was clearly designed for that minuscule creature."

Lola was still trying to get a good look at the huffy dude's face. Wow, what a prick. And to think she'd be stuck next to him for the next five plus hours. She hoped he wasn't like that nutty guy on a plane one time who famously got drunk and pooped on the drinks cart while ranting to the cabin full of freaked-out passengers. This guy would have to climb over her to get there, making things even worse.

At last, a flight attendant showed up with a ticket for his bag and wheeled it away, much to his consternation based on the few choice words he muttered.

"Excuse me," he said, his back still quasi-turned to Lola. She took the hint and squeezed behind him to allow him to sit.

When she slipped back into her seat, she avoided speaking to him, instead stealing a glance from her peripheral vision. Which was when she realized who the jerk was. Her breath caught in her throat.

Omigod omigod omigod, Levi freaking Patton? The asshole making a big scene is my ex-fiancé? Of all the people on the planet to get stuck next to on this flight.

She panicked, wanting to try to hide herself from him

somehow. But where do you hide on a plane? Not like you can even slip off to the bathroom—at some point, the flight attendants would come after you once they knew someone hadn't come out for hours.

Well, this was going to be super awkward. She loosened her seatbelt all the way so she could turn toward the aisle, aiming her back toward him. Which might work till her hip went all pins and needles from being pressed against the seat for so long. Shit. What was she supposed to do?

She reached beneath her seat and pulled the apple from her backpack, then took a big bite from it as she opened her magazine. She forgot to get gum for takeoff so she figured chewing on an apple would serve the same purpose to keep her ears from clogging up. She took another bite, chewing deliberately, then took another.

Then she heard the sound of someone clearing his throat.

She threw a sidelong glance over, desperate to avoid Levi recognizing her.

He cleared his throat again and nodded in her direction. "Would you mind being a little quieter?"

Was he fucking for real? She might have considered Levi a royal douchebag for a long time, but he was never the total dick he was being today. What the hell? She ignored him and took another bite of the apple, chewing a little louder out of spite.

He heaved a sigh, so she figured he'd resigned himself to her noise. Good. After a short while, she noticed he'd put AirPods in and had slumped his head away from her, so she figured the coast was clear—she could at least sit facing forward until she had to get uncomfortable to remain incognito. God, all this to avoid having to interact with Levi Patton after all these years. Though for sure she wondered how he'd become such a curmudgeon. He used to be pretty chill and carefree.

She returned to her magazine and did her best to pretend he wasn't there. Surely, she could dodge the guy for the whole flight—she did that one time with the woman who vomited next to her on a flight to Seattle. Between that woman and Levi, they were on par as far as hazards to avoid.

At some point, she was able to drift off to sleep for a while but was jostled awake when the rude jerk climbed over her to get to the bathroom. Did the man have no manners? She pretended to still be asleep when he came back, and she had her face buried in her hoodie to be sure he wouldn't see it. She stole a glance at her watch to see that she still had three more hours to avoid him. Ugh. Meanwhile, she was bored and hungry and wanted her chips, dammit.

She slunk down and grabbed the bag from beneath her seat, pulling open the package, and started popping chips into her mouth, crunching them as loudly as possible. Oh Lord, Whitney would pee her pants laughing at Lola's antagonistic behavior. If she luck was on her side, maybe he'd hate the smell of barbecue chips too, for good measure.

Sure enough, a few minutes later, the throat clearing resumed. She was growing weary of this. Perhaps she should have it out with him and then she could return to her magazine in peace for the rest of the flight. Not like she wanted to make small talk with him or anything.

She took a deep breath and turned to her seatmate.

"I'm sorry, but do you have something stuck in your throat?"

Levi's eyes bugged open. "Lola?"

Chapter Six

UN-FUCKING-BELIEVABLE. As if this day couldn't get any worse. First the knife roll debacle—Levi couldn't believe he'd forgotten about the damned knives. Everyone knows you can't bring knives on planes! To make matters worse, he knew it was so rude of him to flip his shit on other people over it, but somehow, he couldn't help himself. Ever since the rat tail incident, he'd struggled to keep his temper in check. Which was weird because that never used to be a thing for him. But now, the littlest things set him off.

The whole seat situation didn't help matters. He wanted to rest and relax for a couple of hours and use the many frequent flier points he'd accrued but never had time to use when he was working 24/7. But to lose the upgrade because he had to go back to the check-in desk to send his knives in cargo, well, that was the icing on the shit cake that was his day.

And then he got stuck in the middle next to the noisy seatmate, chewing what sounded like a bag of rocks next to him, only to make him more on edge. It made the hair on his arms stand up on end. Now he knew the mad chewer was none other than the one woman on the planet who'd least want to sit next to him… or even share the same planet. As an added bonus, she got to witness his primo pissy behavior, firsthand. Great. At this point, he hoped the plane would land in one piece, 'cause odds didn't seem to be in his favor today. Maybe it would be best to put him out of his misery. Welp.

He now found himself at cruising altitude some thirty-five-thousand feet above sea level, with the woman he ditched on the day they were planning to elope and marry. What were the chances? And what the hell was he supposed to say to her now?

"So, um… fancy meeting you here?" He shrugged and lifted his hands up.

Lola took a loud bite of a chip, giving a cursory nod. "Levi."

She turned back to her magazine.

Huh. So that's how she was going to play it?

He turned, facing the seat in front of him. But he hadn't downloaded the airline app ahead of time, so he couldn't watch a film. He didn't have any reading material because it was in his carry-on bag, now in the belly of the plane—though with his luck, chances were good it was in the belly of a plane headed to Singapore. All he could do was sit there and stare at the seat in front of him while pretending that his ex-fiancée wasn't next to him, sending out powerful hate vibes in his direction. While revenge-chomping potato chips. Barbecue, no less. Could she have picked something a little less pungent? Especially considering he didn't have time to grab breakfast this morning, having left so late because he'd set his alarm for 4:00 p.m. instead of 4:00 a.m.

Levi closed his eyes and tried to slip off to sleep again, but his brain wasn't having any of that. Instead his mind drifted back to those days, when he and Lola were the opposite of whatever it was they were now. Like, say, passionate lovers who could barely take their hands off of one another. At least it was like that until it wasn't. And when it wasn't, it was all because of him.

How could he deal with the complexities of addressing this on a damn airplane? Impossible, without voices getting loud. And, no doubt, Lola throwing something at him. Deservedly so. He thought back to the last night he'd been with Lola, their bodies twined together on his dinky bed in that ratty little apartment he'd been renting in Northern Virginia... her long, lithe limbs so strong and toned from running cross-country and playing tennis... her soft breasts pressed to his chest, their bodies notched together like they were meant to be that way.

He hadn't known even then, the night before, that he wasn't going to show up the next day at the courthouse. He'd wanted to, of course. Intended to. But then he got that letter from Lola's mother, taped to his door the next morning after Lola had left for class. In it, her mom told Levi he was holding Lola back. That she'd never meet her full potential as long as they were attached at the hip. That Lola was going places, but not if he continued to be an albatross around her neck. Which made him feel extra shitty because wasn't that from some poem in which a sailor kills a big seabird and is forced to wear the carcass around his neck as punishment? That's what her mom thought of him? He would be her punishment for the rest of her life?

He thought about that for a while. Make that, he obsessed on it. As much as he loved Lola—and God, did he ever love her—he could not carry the weight of that burden for all eternity. It would be *his* albatross, knowing he was hers. Talk about a circular firing squad.

So, he no-showed. He was struggling with trying to explain it to Lola without throwing her mother under the bus. No one needed to have that happen, even if her mother deserved it. After all, hadn't she thrown Lola under the bus a bit? It was a whole hot mess of blame and culpability. In

Hard to Get

Levi's mind, it had been so simple: he loved Lola and wanted to make a life with her. Never mind that they were starting out and hadn't finished school and had no money. Or that he lived in a crap apartment. Sure, it wasn't going to be easy. But he hadn't considered that love wasn't enough, at least for the people who mattered most in Lola's world.

It took him a while to compose the text he sent to her. Yeah, he sent a text. In retrospect, that was a lame and cowardly way out. But he also sent a long letter trying to persuade Lola that they both needed to grow up and move on.

He and Lola never spoke again. She refused his calls—he left many messages, unanswered. He heard from others that she'd become good at darts after having put his picture in the center of a dartboard and practiced round the clock to hit the target. Rumor had it there was no image of Levi left—his photo had been turned into a giant hole. At least she developed a skill from her hardship—lemonade from lemons.

Lola was deliberately turned away from Levi now, which gave him a chance to check her out without seeming too creepy. She was even more beautiful than he'd remembered. She still had those sexy-as-shit biceps—if anything, even sexier. And now with a tattoo—of Popeye, of all things. He couldn't decide if that turned him on or made him want to eat spinach. But looking at her brought to the surface the many repressed feelings he'd never lost. Because it wasn't as if he'd fallen out of love with her. Instead he'd cold-turkeyed himself away from her, which hurt, badly.

He looked at his watch. Two hours and forty-five minutes left on this flight. An eternity, under the circumstances. The more he mentally gnawed on things, the more he realized he needed to say something. Clear the air.

It had been long enough. They were both grown-ups. Surely, she had forgiven him by now.

He tapped her on the shoulder, and she turned her head.

"So, you maybe wanna talk about it?" There. He'd said it. How easy was that? He just up and said the words, which were now out there, floating in the ether, waiting for her response.

Lola paused a beat.

"Thanks, but I'd rather chew glass."

She turned back to her magazine.

Well. That backfired. He needed a casual "in." He glanced at what she was reading.

"Ahhh, I see you still love your junky tabloids," he said, with a fake chuckle. "What's happening with Harry and Meghan this week?"

She turned her head toward him and dropped her chin. "You mean the man who married the love of his life despite underlying familial opposition?"

Well, perhaps he should have asked instead about the picture in the corner of Ben Affleck headed back to rehab. Something more neutral.

"About that—"

"You're referring to the *man*"—she put heavy emphasis on the word "man"—"who even uprooted himself, walked away from everything he ever knew, for the woman he loved?"

Oy. This was not going well.

Levi squirmed in his seat. "Look, Lola. I get it. You're still angry with me. But we're stuck in a tin can in the air for few hours with no place to escape to. Can't we be civil and let bygones be bygones?"

She furrowed her brow. "Actually, I'm super happy reading my magazine and eating my Sour Patch Kids and minding my own business. I'm sorry that you forgot to bring something to do on a five-hour flight so you feel compelled instead to resurrect the desiccated cadaver of our relationship to while away the time. Take my advice: if you must spew out some soul-baring confession, I'm sure you can find a Catholic church somewhere when we land in LA with a priest on duty who will listen to your boring story."

With that, she shifted so that her back was facing the center seat again.

Obviously, Levi had underestimated how much Lola hated him.

For the rest of the flight, she stayed in that position until the pilot announced they were beginning their approach to LAX airport, at which point she had no choice but to face front.

Levi reached for his bag but remembered he didn't have one, and thus no pen in his possession. He leaned over to his other seatmate and borrowed one from him, then pulled out a copy of the in-flight magazine and tore off a strip from it and scribbled down his phone number. He figured he'd wait till right before everyone stood up to race off the plane to hand it to Lola. His hand was almost trembling as he worried he might instead trigger a public scene. The last thing he needed at that point was a public scene about anything.

"Here," he said, handing her the scrap of paper. "If you change your mind, you can reach me at this number."

Lola stared at him, then shoved it into the now-closed magazine. "Whatever."

He heard the telltale chimes and anyone with an aisle seat raced to get up and grab their bags from the overhead bins, officially ending any more chance of conversation with Lola Quigley, ex-fiancée and all-around pissed-off woman.

Chapter Seven

THAT man had some nerve, Lola thought. First off, trying to make nice after all these years, on a damned airplane no less. As if she would air nearly a decade's worth of dirty laundry with a huge captive audience.

And second, curse him for looking so freaking hot still, proving once again that there is no justice in the world. After what he'd done to her, Lola had hoped her voodoo doll efforts and dart skills would have somehow affected him. Like maybe super bad acne on his face similar to the puncture holes in his picture. Maybe a bad limp from where she'd stuck the pins into the doll. Something. But no. He was too handsome, with that wavy brown hair she used to love to weave her fingers through and those molten-brown puppy dog eyes that made you want to forgive all his transgressions because he looked so earnest.

She'd surprised herself with her own restraint. Because most every molecule in her body kinda wanted to lick his face and tell him all was forgiven. But she wasn't the same Lola that he knew. She was strong Lola. Kick-ass Lola. Take-no-prisoners Lola. She glanced at her arm as she flexed her bicep, watching her Popeye tattoo appear to move. When she was a little girl, her grandpa used to squeeze her scrawny little arm and tell her if she ate all of her vegetables she'd grow up to be strong like Popeye, that guy from the cartoon with the bulging biceps thanks to all his spinach consumption.

When she broke down after Levi abandoned her, her grandfather was there to remind her she was as strong as Popeye and could make it through anything. And she did make it through the darkness, and she got the tattoo to remind herself of that accomplishment. She was strong and smart and skilled and could do anything she set her mind to. Right now, that meant winning *Shop till you Drop*. So, she had to put all things Levi out of her mind at once because she would never see him again and he was a big fat nothing in her life anyhow. Even if he was too damned handsome for his own good.

Lola grabbed an Uber to her hotel and upon arrival, unpacked right away, then sprawled out on the comfy king-sized bed, propped up against a mountain of down pillows. This show spared no expenses on their chosen chefs, which was reassuring. She'd been informed there was a 6:30 a.m. call time for the next morning, and she half wanted to explore LA for a few hours, but she was exhausted from an early morning already and had no clue how exhausting tomorrow would be. Instead she ordered up room service, pulled up a rom-com on Netflix, and went to bed on East Coast time.

All contestants were scheduled to meet in the lobby and ride together in a van to the studio. The producer, Amy Ming, a petite twenty-something young woman with an adorable black bob, was there to make introductions, giving Lola her first chance to size up the competition.

First she met Andre, a lanky, bearded food truck chef from New Mexico who seemed nice enough. Then the heavily tatted Bettina, a caterer who wore the shortest skirt she'd ever seen and sky-high heels, which Lola couldn't imagine she would wear while cooking. Maybe she was trying to woo the judges with her hot bod. Ugh. There was a retired chef named Jonathan who was about her grandfather's age and moved at a slow pace—it looked like he wasn't going to give her much of a run for her money. And last came Ariana, an LA native fresh out of culinary school who reminded everyone of that almost every time she opened her mouth.

"I'm surprised there are five of us—aren't there usually more?" Lola asked.

Amy grinned. "Glad you asked. We've got a little surprise we're cooking up for you this time."

Lola lifted her brow. "A surprise? When do we learn what it is?"

"In due time," Amy said. "But let's get you set up in your trailers and soon enough you'll learn more."

The van pulled up in front of a large warehouse. Amy led them inside to what turned out to be an enormous grocery store, expressly there for the television show and nothing else. As she glanced down some of the aisles, she saw ingredients you couldn't dream of finding at your average grocery store: cans of escargots, quark, za'atar, yuzu, barberries, 'nduja, gochujang, and epazote. This was a dream grocery store for a girl like Lola. She was gonna fit right in here.

There were five cooking stations set up along one side of the cash register area at the front of the set and one other station on an elevated platform on the other side.

"Is that the throne I get to cook at when I win it all?" said a beaming Ariana, the newly minted chef, who Lola made a mental note to refer to as the Fresh Chef of Bel Air. Lola noticed that Bettina threw her the stink eye.

Amy wagged her finger. "That's for later on." She motioned for them to follow her toward the back of the store, where a door led to a set of trailers in a parking lot. Each one had a name attached to it, and she pointed each contestant to their respective trailers. "That's going to be your home while here. You need to remain inside your trailer at all times. If you need something, there's a phone right inside the door—lift it up and someone will answer and help you out. Either I or one of our production assistants will come get you when it's time to Shop till You Drop!"

Ariana let out a squeal of excitement; Bettina whistled like she was calling for a lost dog. Jonathan clapped politely and Andre did a little celebratory fist bump. Lola gulped hard.

Her trailer was stocked with food and drink and had a large flat-screen television set to previous episodes of *Shop till you Drop*. She wasn't sure if this might make her feel sick to her stomach or help refresh her memory for winning strategies. After all, she'd watched every episode she could find over and over till she could recite the contestants' words verbatim.

Instead, she decided to lie on the floor and practice a little mindfulness breathing. It turned out to be useful because she ended up nodding off, which turned out to be a nice, soothing way to while away what otherwise would have seemed like an eternity. But before she knew it, she heard a knock on her door: Amy had come to retrieve her.

"So, I'm going to introduce you all to our host, Martin Palumbo, and he'll go over the rules, which you all know, and then he will tell you the first game. You ready?"

"As I'll ever be, I guess," Lola said.

"You feel comfortable with your competition?"

Lola nodded. "Seems like we're all pretty evenly matched."

Amy winked. "It'll be interesting to find out, won't it?"

Lola squinted. Huh. That sounded cryptic. It would be interesting indeed.

Chapter Eight

LEVI arrived at the studio at nine o'clock as prompted and got the full tour of the studio with the producer, that Amy Ming woman.

"So the contestants don't know about you yet, and they don't know that they're basically cooking against you," she said. "They'll have a big surprise when we introduce you."

Levi could only imagine how thrilled they'd all be to meet him. Bad enough to be pitted against competition you know, but when it's a chef—a once highly vaunted chef at that—it would be far worse. Even if his name was dirt, he could still cook the pants off of most others in the kitchen.

"I want you to meet our host." She reached for a large guy with a bit of a beer gut standing near a camera operator. "Marty, you need to meet Levi Patton. Levi, this is Marty."

"Levi, dude." Marty's hand swooped in for one of those big man grips that made Levi fear for his chopping hand. "Wanted you to know how bad I feel about it all."

It all. This was the part that made Levi cringe. He was such a pariah in the food world, even on a hokey show like *Shop till you Drop*. He knew things were bad when cheeseballs from reality cooking shows were shoveling out the false empathy.

Levi shrugged. "Thanks." What else could he say?

"I know you'll make us proud here, hopefully vindicate yourself a bit."

Hard to vindicate oneself from a rat tail in your soup by going on a reality cooking show, but what did he know?

"Yeah, well."

Luckily Amy chose that awkward moment to hasten him away to his trailer.

"I'll be back for you shortly!"

Shortly ended up being a good ninety minutes. This time when Amy escorted him back to the warehouse grocery store, he entered through a different door and, in an instant, the cameras were aimed at him.

"Go get 'em, tiger," Amy said as she gave him a gentle shove toward the bright lights.

Levi could hear Marty introducing him.

"He was the rising star hipster chef-owner of the most popular restaurant in Washington, DC, until he served a bouillabaisse to a food critic with a little rat tail garnish," Palumbo said. "Let's give it up for Levi Patton, a talented chef who's here trying to rehabilitate his career, and I know you'll all love him. Who doesn't love a good comeback story?"

Well, fuck. He hadn't expected to be the poster child for pity parties, but it was clear this was what they'd intended with him. He took a deep breath, wiped the sweat from his palms, and ran down the aisle as if he gave one flying fuck about being on this show. If nothing else, they should consider him for an Academy Award for this acting job.

He sidled up to Marty for a dose of happy talk.

"Levi, so great to see you, fella," he said, giving him a hearty pat on the back. "You ready to play this game?"

Levi pasted on a grin. "As ready as I'll ever be, I guess."

"First, I'll explain the rules of the game: each contestant will choose two unusual ingredients at random from this shopping cart," he said. "All of these are foods that various food banks have reportedly received as donations. Let's just say, not your average can of pork and beans." He gave a smirk. "Once you've gotten your two items, you have thirty minutes to produce a meal for our judges to enjoy."

To enjoy at my expense, Levi thought.

"Let's get going and meet your contestants! First, we have Andre from Santa Fe, whose food truck won best of the year two years running. Next Bettina, a caterer with a flair for fashion. Jonathan, a retired chef with four grandchildren rooting him on from home. Ariana, an LA native fresh from culinary school and an internship with Wolfgang Puck. Last we have Lola, who, in her spare time, fixes meals for homeless folks in her DC community."

Levi glared into the lights as he tried to make out the faces of the chefs he'd be pitted against. He saw a tall bearded dude and a shorter gal with a crap ton of tattoos up and down her arms and legs and even on her neck. An older gentleman with pronounced white bobcat-like eyebrows looked like a nice grandpa. Next was a thin, nervous-looking woman with bushy red hair. The last woman stood at the far end, and as he squinted, he realized that by Lola, Marty meant *Lola*. Lola who gave him the burn on the plane. Was that only yesterday? Lola? Here? What the hell was she doing on this show?

He squinted at her and mouthed, "Huh?"

She curled her lip back.

Well, for fuck's sake. This was turning out to be even worse than he'd expected, and it hadn't even started yet.

Maybe he'd be lucky and the judges would find some unwanted animal body part in his first dish and send him packing. It would be precisely what he deserved.

Chapter Nine

LOLA felt the blood drain from her face the minute she saw who the big damned surprise was. Jesus H. Christ. How on earth could she be competing on a show with him? How was he a chef? How was he a chef who lost everything over a rat tail? How was she going to compete against someone like him and win?

Her head felt so woozy it was hard to hear what Martin Palumbo was saying. It was all so muffled and far away. That's when she hit the floor. And then someone was smacking her face, and she was on her back on the floor, the powerful smell of ammonia permeating her olfactory system.

"Hey, Lola, it's me, Amy. You okay? We've called for paramedics. They'll be here any minute."

Lola was still a little confused, but the idea of paramedics coming for her seemed crazy. Why? She started collecting her thoughts: the show, the hot lights, her nerves, and the revelation that Levi was the guest competitor. Levi who she didn't even know was a chef, let alone one who was shamed out of his profession.

"I don't need any medical care. I'm fine, really," she said. "I think I was dehydrated, and my nerves got to me and—"

Martin clapped his hands. "Okay, everybody, let's take a thirty-minute break and we'll start again then."

He reached a hand down to help Lola up. "Let's get you

some water and a little food and you can rest for a few minutes."

"We'll have to shoot that all again, though?"

He shook his head. "Oh, hell no! That was ratings gold there, my friend."

"But I passed out."

"You sure did. The audience will love it. You'll have a built-in fan base because of it too."

"I don't want people to take pity on me!"

"Sweetheart, any way you can single yourself out from a crowd is a good thing. Now up, up." He clapped his hands as he motioned for her to get moving. "Time's a-wasting."

To add to her embarrassment, Amy insisted on having two strong cameramen escort Lola back to her trailer, one on each arm. Talk about being mortified.

Lola drank the carton of orange juice that someone insisted would help her blood sugar levels as she sat on the comfy sofa in her trailer watching *Shop till you Drop* for lack of anything better to do during this brief break in the action. God, showing back up on the set would be so embarrassing. What a schmuck.

She heard a light rap on the door and called for whoever it was to come in. She heard the door shut and a throat being cleared and ugh, it was déjà vu all over again.

"Lola?"

She rolled her eyes. "What are you doing here? I mean seriously, why are you here ruining my life all over again?"

He stepped forward till he was next to the sofa. "May

I?" He motioned toward the seat.

"Fine. Whatever."

He took a seat next to her. "Are you doing okay? When you passed out like that, it worried me."

"Yeah, well, when your ex-fiancé intrudes on your life not once but twice in a week and on the most important day of your life—make that the second most important day because conveniently, he failed to show up for the most important one—well, it sometimes leads to an emotional meltdown. Of sorts."

"Look, Lola, I know this is not the time or the place to delve into everything. It's so complicated and it was a long time ago. So much has happened in the ensuing years. But I hope you can accept that I'm sorry and that the last thing I want to be is a continual thorn in your side right now." He raked his fingers through his hair. "As you might have guessed, it's not the best of times for me either. I'm not looking for your pity or anything—I say that to let you know I'm only doing what's necessary to keep my head above water right now."

Lola frowned. "Shit, Levi. What was up with the rat tail thing? I mean, I can't believe I didn't even know you were some big-deal chef. Kinda nuts. But what went wrong?"

He splayed his legs out and leaned back against the sofa. "It blindsided me. Things were going great. My restaurant was doing great—lines out the door every night. One night, I knew the guy who'd come in was the food critic from the *Chronicle*. I checked every item of food myself before it left the kitchen that night. Everything. A couple of folks in the kitchen told me they thought it was a jealous sous chef who sabotaged me. But I could never prove it. In the blink of an eye, I went from up here"—he held his hand above his head—"to down here." He reached toward the floor. "The most meteoric crash in DC restaurant history, the papers said. From lines out the door, to I couldn't give my food away to a homeless person on the street."

"I beg to differ with that," she said.

He lifted a brow. "What do you mean?"

"'Cause I was pretty close to that myself for a while, and I took any food people offered me."

He squinted at her. "You were homeless?"

She sighed and leaned back against the sofa as well. "When things, well, when it all happened, it pretty much broke my spirit. I kind of stopped functioning. I stopped going to school, I gave up my part-time job, I lost my lease. I gave up."

Levi closed his eyes. He couldn't bear to hear this. "All because of me?"

She frowned and nodded. "Pretty much so."

"But I did what your mother told me was best for you."

She turned her head to look at him. "What do you mean?"

"Crap. I didn't intend to share that with you."

"Share what with me?"

"What I just said."

"You need to elaborate."

He shook his head. "I loved you so much and was all set to marry you—you know that. But then your mother left this note on my door that morning telling me I would ruin your life if I married you. That you had all of these great things before you and being married to me would thwart that. She said if I loved you, I'd let you go."

Lola's eyes grew wide. "My mother said that to you?"

"Well, in a letter."

"If she wasn't already dead, I swear to God, I'd kill her." Lola took a deep breath. "My mother was always so jealous of my relationship with you. I could tell, you know. She pretended to embrace it around me, but then she'd make caustic remarks also, subtle ways to undermine me, things like how you were never going to make anything of yourself. That you would hold me back."

"Well, looks like she was right. I'm a big fat nothing, same as she predicted."

She smacked his arm. "Stop it. That's nonsense. Look at you in your fancy chef's coat. You're a big deal."

"Was a big deal. Now I'm the laughingstock of the industry. I only came on this show out of desperation."

"I'm sorry," she said, placing her hand on his. "Even more so because I'm kind of desperate here too. I need to win this badly."

There was a loud knock on the door. "Back to the studio, everybody! Five minutes!"

"Oh crap," he said. "We're probably not even supposed to be together. Look, you go on ahead of me and I'll follow in a few after the coast is clear. Maybe we can talk more later?"

Lola bit her lip. "I don't know. Let's see how things go, 'k?"

He nodded. Why did he expect anything otherwise? It's not like she'd forget everything and pretend they were back where they were ten years ago. They were both here with competing goals; they couldn't simply pick up where they left off. He would have to resign himself to that.

Chapter Ten

LOLA hated that everyone kept pandering to her, checking that she was all right. All she wanted was to get this thing started so everyone could forget about her fainting and so she could forget the conversation with Levi, which turned everything she'd ever believed on its head. At some point, she'd ponder all of that, but right now, she needed to clear her head and focus on the task in front of her.

"Okay, contestants, in the first round you're going to spin this wheel to see what two ingredients you have to use to prepare your entrée. Lola, in honor of your delicate state, I'm giving you the first spin."

Lola winced. *Delicate state my ass…*

She stepped up to the wheel and gave it a spin, and it landed on soaked bamboo leaves. Okay, bamboo leaves. She could work with that. Her second spin gave her precooked sticky rice. Perfect. She knew exactly what to do with this.

Her fellow competitors spun the wheel and landed on some dubious ingredients: canned abalone and Spam, for instance. One of Levi's ingredients was canned jumbo squid. At least she'd lucked into something workable.

The competitors lined up behind their shopping carts and on the count of three, Marty waved a checkered flag—talk about drama—and they were off, elbowing each other out of the way to find the ingredients they needed ASAP.

For Lola, the first thing that came to mind was a speed

version of joong, a dish traditionally eaten during the Dragon Boat Festival, a big holiday in Chinese culture from what she'd learned on an Instagram story last week. Joong was like a dumpling minus the skin. And while she was sure there were plenty of traditional ingredients used in it, for her purposes it was about to become more like a freestyle chimichanga—what the chef at the Mexican restaurant she used to work at called the "garbage bucket." On second thought, maybe it was more comparable to a tamale. Either which way, she had a lot to accomplish in the next thirty minutes.

First stop, the international food aisle, where she grabbed dried shrimp and dried scallops for some umami, along with a can of water chestnuts and a vacuum-sealed package of cooked, salted duck egg yolks. Then to the meat section where she was pleasantly surprised to find a sous vide pork belly, all ready and waiting for her to do something with it. She grabbed some pork, garlic, and ginger sausages, which would have a nice Asian flare. She rounded off her shopping with a handful of dried shiitake mushrooms, a can of corn, a jar of pimentos, and some plain dental floss to wrap the bamboo leaves. Maybe it wasn't common to use pimentos for joong, but she liked the added color.

She returned to her station within a few quick minutes and got to work preparing her dish. To save chopping them, she crunched the dried shiitakes into bits and dropped them into hot water to hydrate. In a flash, she heated the oil in a wok, chopped the pork belly into bite-sized pieces, and tossed them in to give a little caramelization to the meat. It was already cooked but needed that extra bit. Next she gave the sticky rice a quick stir-fry to heat it up and mixed the peanuts in with it, along with a handful of drained corn and pimentos. Setting that aside, she chopped the sausages into one-inch pieces, laid out all her ingredients in bowls, and spread out the bamboo leaves. After that, she began the delicate process of assembling the joong, making sure not to crack the leaf as she placed a layer of the rice mixture first into the delicate pocket secured in her palm, added the tiny shrimp and scallops, both meats, an egg yolk on either side, and some sprinkles of the drained mushrooms, then topped it with another rice layer.

Next she flapped the bamboo leaves over the palm-sized serving of ingredients, sealing the top and sides. She grabbed her dental floss to start quickly wrapping the three-inch-long packages and popped them into an Instant Pot, covering them with water. She set the timer and hoped for the best.

Meanwhile, she hadn't thought about the idle time while they cooked, so she grabbed her cart and hunted down ingredients to throw together a simple Asian salad to accompany the joong. She tossed into the cart a head of Napa cabbage and red cabbage, carrots, a bunch of scallions, shelled edamame, sriracha sauce, soy sauce, honey, and rice wine vinegar.

She zipped back to her station and checked the timer on her Instant Pot, then set to work shredding cabbage, slicing scallions and matchstick pieces of carrot, and whipping together a simple dressing. She wasn't going to win any awards with this salad, but she thought it would help with the overall presentation of her dish. Plus, she could plate this salad while she waited for the joong to finish cooking.

"Okay, chefs, we've got five minutes left on the clock," Marty said.

Lola's heart was racing in her throat, she was so anxious. She glanced up to see the rest of her competition looked equally unnerved, beads of sweat on their foreheads and looks of panic on their faces. Except for Levi, who looked like nothing fazed him. Her Instant Pot dinged and she grabbed the lid and opened it, barely dodging the plume of steam it emitted. With tongs she grabbed her joong from the pot, placing one on each of the three judges' plates with care. She drizzled the dressing on top of the salad just as Marty told them time was up. All chefs stopped what they were doing and held their hands up in the air.

Marty rubbed his hands together. "Okay, folks, looks like you handled that first try pretty handily. You ready for the judges to sample your wares?"

They all nodded obligingly. Lola wiped her sweaty palms on her apron and took a deep breath.

One by one, the judges critiqued the food prepared by each contestant. Poor Ariana got slammed for her ostrich egg omelet with pickled pigs' feet—overcooked and rubbery. Lola felt a little sorry for her as she saw a trickle of tears course down her cheeks. This competitive cooking was not for the fainthearted.

Finally, it was her turn.

"What does our delicate little flower have for the judges?" Martin asked.

God, she wanted to slug him for kicking that dead horse. Enough with the fragile Lola thing.

She smiled a constipated smile.

"I've prepared a twist on joong, a traditional Chinese food eaten during the Dragon Boat Festival each year. Obviously, I had to tweak it due to time constraints. I hope you like it."

Lola blushed. She hated being the center of attention and this was that on steroids. She couldn't bring herself to look past the judges' table to see how the other contestants reacted.

Hard to Get

Lola hadn't a clue who the judges even were. The little signs in front of them displayed their names, but she wasn't hep to the world of competitive cooking, so they could have been anyone. The first judge, a woman, weighed in.

"Dayum, that's delicious," she said, licking her fork. "It felt like Christmas opening this package and anticipating the flavors inside. And you did not disappoint."

"I agree—delectable," said a male judge with a double chin that attested to his love of food.

The third judge made her nervous—an Asian woman who she feared might have a much better idea about how these should taste.

She paused before commenting, taking another bite. "I have to tell you," she said. Lola braced for the worst. "I loved the irreverent addition of corn and pimentos, not something my grandma and mother put in their joong—also known as zongzi. I would've liked more depth of flavor with the pork, but I know that joong is something that takes days to prepare, so given the time constraints, I'll let that slide. Nice work."

Lola breathed a sigh of relief. She thought the judges were receptive enough for her to make it through to the next round.

"Okay, judges, if you want to put your heads together, it's time to figure out who you're sending home," Marty said as he walked station to station, sampling what each cook had prepared. "Nice work, Orchid."

"Orchid?"

"Ba-ha-ha! I was trying to come up with a delicate flower." He gave her a wink.

Oy. Lola was going to have to ride this horse in the direction it was galloping. She needed Marty on her side, so if he was obsessed with his stupid corny jokes, he could have at it. She was too strong to be kneecapped by that stuff.

She forced out a little laugh and decided it wasn't a big deal to laugh with him, even if it might have felt like it was at her expense.

He dug a fork into Levi's squid carpaccio—which the judges of course adored—and gave him the thumbs-up sign as he chewed away. Lola needed to keep her eyes on the prize. She had to beat Levi to win this competition, which meant she had her work cut out for her.

"Judges, what do you have for us?" Marty asked, returning to face the panel.

"It was a tough decision," the male judge said. Andre's root beer-infused Vienna sausages were pretty darned creative, and I think we all liked that."

"I thought Lola's joong was quite a brave take on something that Chinese grandmothers and moms and aunties have been preparing traditionally forever. It's hard to impress me with that, but she hit the nail on the head."

Phew. That was a ringing endorsement.

"Honestly, we weren't blown away by Bettina's canned pasta casserole, and I'm afraid Ariana's omelet lacked on so many levels."

"So, which two chefs are we saying goodbye to?"

The woman lifted the cover over both the ostrich omelet and Bettina's pasta dish as a loud buzzer sounded. Sayonara to Ariana and Bettina, thank goodness!

Marty escorted the two women off-stage and returned.

"Okay, remaining contestants: we've got two more chefs to be eliminated in this next round, and then it comes down to the remaining two. I'll give you a forty-five-minute break while we reset the stage here, and we'll get back to it."

Lola heaved a sigh of relief. She could go recharge her batteries and not think about anything until she had to.

Hard to Get

Good luck with that.

Chapter Eleven

LEVI had to admit he was pretty impressed with Lola's cooking on the fly. How on earth had she developed those cooking skills? He was desperate to know. And he was desperate to slip back to her trailer to talk to her some more. Would she welcome it, or would approaching her push him away?

Hell, he didn't know if he'd make it past the next round. If he was eliminated, that would be it—he'd never see her again. He needed to carpe diem while he could. He slipped out the trailer door, making sure there was no one else around looking, and walked five trailers down to Lola's, knocking lightly.

"Enter," a voice said.

He walked in and stood by the door again, waiting for an invitation to sit. This time she wasn't on the sofa.

"Lola?" he called out.

"Back here."

He followed her voice and found her sprawled out on a bed. He hadn't even investigated his own trailer enough to know there was a bed there. Well, this could be awkward.

"Hey," he said, looking down at the floor. "Congratulations on your exceptional debut. Looks like you've made quite an impression on the judges."

"You think?"

"I don't just think, I know. Judges on food shows don't

blow smoke up your ass. If they don't like something, you're gonna hear it and hear it loud."

She shrugged. "Cool. Still a lot of hurdles to overcome though."

A quick glance around the room told him there was no place to sit. He took it upon himself and perched on the smallest corner of the bed possible. Otherwise, it was too weird to tower over her.

"Can I ask you something?"

"Yeah, sure," she said.

"How did you develop your mad cooking skills?"

"I could ask you the same thing."

"But I asked you first."

"But I have a greater need for answers right now than you do."

He shrugged. He couldn't argue with that.

"So after... after everything..." He pursed his lips for a moment and continued. "I was a bit of a lost soul. I'd hurt the person who mattered most to me in the world but was told I had to hurt her to do the right thing." He shook his head. "I felt like the worst person on the planet. And seriously, I was a kid. I wasn't prepared to handle this kind of emotional burden. So, I kind of shut down. I decided to do some sort of penance for my actions and started working the worst kinds of jobs. It was like those monks who self-flagellate, lashing their backs with heavy chains. Only instead, I took a job cleaning out porta-potties."

Lola's eyes grew wide. "You're kidding, right?"

He shook his head. "If only. I wasn't particularly imaginative in coming up with good punishments, was I?"

"I'd have said weeding would have been ample enough torment. Cleaning out portable toilets was way beyond the call of duty."

"I should have solicited that advice." He chuckled. "'Cause, well, yeah. It was a pretty shitty job." He grinned.

"Literally." She stuck out her tongue like she was gagging.

"Needless to say, I didn't last long in that gig. Next up, I started working as a dishwasher. Oh, and I forgot. I up and moved to New York City. I lived in a boardinghouse in a rough neighborhood and started doing dishes at one of the most popular restaurants in the city."

"At least it was a step up. You were still cleaning up messes, but they were a little more palatable."

"Yeah, and if you hang around a kitchen and you've got some ambition, you can learn a lot," he said. "Eventually I started working my way up. I was a porter, I did prep work, and after a few years, I worked my way up to line cook. By then, I knew it was my calling. After I hopped around for a while, I came back to DC and opened my own place. I had no clue it was going to be such a huge success. It kind of happened accidentally."

"Doesn't sound all that accidental."

"Hey, enough about me. I wanted to tell you how impressed I was with your cooking today. I'd share a kitchen with you any day."

She smiled. "High praise from the likes of someone with your level of skill."

"I'm serious. It was kind of a turn-on watching you out there going about your business, cranking out that food like it was nothing. You were a machine, totally focused on what you were doing."

Lola rolled over to face him. "A turn-on? For real? I never thought about cooking like that."

"I don't know if it's cooking or your commanding presence, but you came across as large and in charge. I liked that. It was kind of exciting to watch."

"So, while I was cooking you were watching me?"

He inched his way a little farther onto the bed. "Sorta hard not to, Lol. I mean, first off, every time I watched Popeye flex—"

She laughed. "Heh. You like my tat?"

"It's awesome. What made you get it?"

She closed her eyes, seemingly lost in thought for a minute. "After, well, after everything, I was a hot mess. I kind of couldn't get my shit together. I couldn't do school, I couldn't relax. I couldn't do anything. Even sitting still was awful because it made me think about things even more. I didn't want to think about things at all."

A tear formed in the corner of her eye and it about killed him. He couldn't help himself—he slipped down along the mattress, facing Lola. He reached out and stroked her hair with his fingers. "I'm sorry, Lol. I'm so sorry."

She let out a sob and he pulled her face to his chest. Shit, this was not what they should be doing right now. They should be mentally preparing for the next round, not having an emotional bloodletting. But he needed it and suspected she did even more.

"All I could think of was 'why?' Why did you do that to me? Why would you evaporate from my life like that? My mother kept telling me to buck up. That I deserved better than you, that you'd never make anything of yourself. That stuff didn't help me. I needed to stop dwelling on you and instead focus on me."

"So what did you do?"

"I languished. For a long while. I dropped out of school. Moved away from my mother, who had become too toxic for me. I took a bunch of awful jobs and could barely afford my rent. I was on food stamps. I took donations from food banks and soup kitchens. And I learned to do something with next to nothing. I found out I had a talent for creating magic with some lousy food products."

She looked up at him and grinned. He wiped her tears with his thumb.

"I'm sorry, Lola. I'm so, so sorry." He pulled her toward him again.

They lay there like that for silent minutes, the sound of their breathing all he could notice.

"It's okay, Levi. Don't sweat it."

How could he not? This was all his doing. Because he was so foolish as to believe her mom.

"So, my grandpa pretty much took me under his wing after my mom died."

"What happened to her?"

"Aneurism. The doctors said she was dead in an instant."

"How old were you?"

"Twenty-one."

"Oh, Lol."

"You know things weren't great between my mom and me. She had a mean streak in her, especially when she was drunk. She always blamed my father for leaving her. Said it was his fault she was so mean."

"But you had your grandpa."

"When I was little, he'd joke around with me and squeeze my scrawny arms and tell me if I ate my vegetables I'd grow up strong like Popeye. When things were at their worst, he always reminded me that I was strong, like Popeye, and that I'd make it through the darkest time."

Levi's heart ached for Lola's pain. He wished there was something he could do to make it up to her. And so he did the one thing his instincts were telling him to do: he pulled her chin toward his with his pointer finger, placing his lips against hers ever so softly, waiting to see if she'd reject him. When she didn't turn away, he followed her cue and pressed his lips to hers more firmly. Folding her body into his, he swept his tongue along her lips, hoping she'd let him give her a proper kiss.

Her tongue met his and tangled with it as they both probed and explored one another's mouths. It was at once the most natural feeling in the world and something magical and new. Levi couldn't understand the feelings washing over him, but he knew it was right. His hands smoothed along her body, her sides, and down her back, and he pulled her closer with his hands on her well-shaped bottom. As he became braver, his hands skimmed around to the front, sliding beneath her T-shirt, and settled over her soft breasts. He couldn't believe he was here, now, this close to Lola after all these years.

"Oh God, Lola, baby," he said.

She moaned when he pinched her nipples through the silky bra. His brain could focus solely on this: wanting to be one with Lola Quigley, the girl he let get away so long ago.

He released the kiss to lift her shirt over her head, then popped the latch to her bra. He could only stare in awe as her breasts spilled out for him to see. It took his breath away. Leaning forward, he flicked his tongue along first one nipple, then the other. He couldn't believe that he was here, sucking on Lola's breast as if no time had passed. He pulled one nipple into his mouth while he toyed with the other. Her moans were his undoing.

"Fuck, Lola." He reached down and, in a rush, undid the button on her jeans, zipping down the fly. With one hand tugging her pants down, he took her panties with them. He wanted to feel himself deep inside her body more than he wanted to take another breath, but he also knew he had to take his time, give her a chance to get used to this. So, he shimmied down her body, licking a path from her breast to her belly and farther down to her neatly trimmed pussy.

"Oh, babe, it's perfect," was all he could say as he settled between her spread legs and stroked his tongue along her folds, relishing the gasps she let loose. As he took long, slow licks along her wet lips, he watched her face contort in pleasure. He inserted a finger inside of her channel, slick with her juices, and hooked it to reach that perfect spot he knew would bring her to climax. Stroking his tongue along her lips, he circled her swollen clit again and again while his finger worked her to orgasm. Her muscles clamped down around his finger, her body spasmed, and she moaned his name out loud. He'd never been this satisfied with a woman without even removing his clothes. As her body fluttered down from her sexual climax, he licked her clean, then scooted himself up so they were face-to-face.

"Would you mind if I kissed you again?" he said. "If memory serves me right, you didn't mind licking your juices from my mouth."

Loud pounding on the door broke the mood. "Five minutes!"

Well, crap. Talk about coitus interruptus.

Lola closed her eyes and shook her head as if waking from a dream. "Oh God, this has to stop. You're not even supposed to be here." She hopped off the bed and pulled her clothes back on.

"Can we talk some more when we're done?" Levi was hopeful but doubtful. The spell had been broken, and he could sense she'd retreated into some other place that didn't include Levi Patton anymore.

Chapter Twelve

ON the one hand, there was nothing like a good orgasm to clear the mind. On the other, this one did nothing but muddy things up a ton. Lola had started the day with her ex-fiancé parked squarely in the corner of "shittiest man on the planet" status. And yet here she stood, after his mouth and hands had worked her to climax with great ease not ten minutes earlier, and she couldn't figure out what he was to her now. Except that he was, for sure, a competitor—the most important obstacle between them.

All that other stuff hadn't gone away. She needed time, though, to digest everything and figure out what was in her heart and mind. Nevertheless, she had to steer clear from Levi Patton because she had goals, and he stood in the way of the most important one. She decided to ignore how amazing it felt to be with him like that; she hadn't been with a man in so long she'd forgotten the last time, so it had to be a purely a biological thing.

Focus, Lola. You've got to focus.

"You feeling all right, Orchid?" Marty said, fake punching her in the Popeye. "You look a little woozy."

God, if he only knew.

"Doing great, Marty old boy." She punched him back.

"Great. We don't want you face-planting again—our floors can't take the dents."

Everyone got a little chuckle out of that. Lola simply

smiled. Nothing was getting in the way of her winning this thing.

"Listen up, people," Marty continued. "This time you'll have a ping-pong ball pop up from this machine and you grab the ball, and written on that ball will be your ingredients. Once again, you'll get two balls."

Heh. "Two balls" made Lola think of blue balls and for a second, she felt awful for poor Levi. He couldn't be feeling too awesome right now, having not had the courtesy orgasm he deserved after the one he gave her. She had yet to figure out if she intended to return the favor. The horny part of her was prepared to. But her wounded psyche left her still confused and trying to understand where the two of them stood—besides being completely upended.

Meanwhile, lost in thought, she missed both Jonathan's and Andre's selections. Marty was about to give Levi first pick, but he deferred.

"Please, let the lady have her choice first," he said, extending his arm.

Make that the lady who'd just enjoyed a good old-fashioned tongue-lashing of sorts, from him. Lola blushed as Levi winked at her.

Marty turned the machine back on and she grabbed for a ball, then read it. "Canned tuna," she said. That would be super easy. The next one was stinging nettles. Which she knew about because her grandpa had taught her when she was little how to handle stinging nettles to make soup. This would be a breeze: a simple linguine dish with tuna and stinging nettle pesto.

"On your mark, get set, go," Marty said, waving that silly flag again as they hit the aisles in search of necessary ingredients.

First destination: latex gloves. Without them, those

nettles would indeed be stinging. In the produce aisle she grabbed fresh mint, garlic, and a couple of lemons. After that, she grabbed some duck eggs, durum wheat and doppio zero flours, along with some semolina flour. To make it over the top, she planned to make a fresh batch of pasta. Next a chunk of parmigiano, a jar of pine nuts, and a can of cannellini beans as an added bonus, and she was back at her station.

First up, she put a pot of salted water on the stove to boil. Then she filled a pot with cold water, and with gloved hands, submerged the nettles and let them sit. Keeping the gloves on, she weighed and mixed the two finer flours, spread the mixture out on her prep surface, and made a well in the middle into which she cracked her duck eggs. Slowly she stirred the eggs, incorporating them into the flour while she added the salt. Once the mixture was blended, she kneaded the dough, then wrapped it in plastic and tucked it into the fridge.

Back to the nettles, she removed them from the pot and drained the water. Separating the leaves, she discarded the stems. She dropped the leaves into the salted water for one minute, drained them, and spread them out on a baking sheet, squeezing out as much water as possible. After chopping them, she placed them in the bowl of her food processor along with the mint, garlic, pine nuts, and lemon juice, pulsing them till they formed a paste. She streamed in some olive oil, transferred it all to a bowl, grated the cheese in, and seasoned with salt and pepper.

Grabbing the pasta dough from the fridge, she rolled it out in seconds and fed it through the pasta machine, bunching each batch into small balls. Immediately, she dropped them into the pasta cooker, draining and tossing to coat it with her pesto and stirring the cannellini beans in. She plated the judges' servings as Marty called time.

The judges thought that Andre's canned corned beef hash burger didn't have any real creativity behind it. One judge gave Jonathan props for his sauerkraut gnocchi, but the other two declared it inedible. They all adored Levi's canned alligator meat chili and gave him kudos for incorporating the bittersweet chocolate into it so successfully.

Finally, it came time for Lola's food to be judged.

"I've always had a fear of stinging nettles since falling into a bed of them when I was a little boy," the one judge said. "But you have done yourself proud and made me a convert with this simple yet remarkable dish. Brava." The other two judges were equally pleased.

"Judges, which two chefs will be heading home?" Marty said.

Lola almost peed herself with excitement when she didn't see her dish revealed. And when she realized it was down to her and Levi, her palms began to sweat.

"Well, it looks like we have the flat-out amateur and the ultimate professional in the final round of play," Marty said. "Orchid, what do you plan to do with the money if you win?"

"So, I've been working to feed homeless people in DC for a while now and have wanted to start a soup kitchen food truck. But it takes money. A lot of money. So that's what I would do with my winnings."

Marty nodded. "Ahhh, we have a big-hearted cook amongst us." He turned to Levi. "Chef, what are your plans?"

Levi froze. "I, well, huh. I guess. Uh, I hadn't thought about that to be honest. Since things, uh, happened at my restaurant, I've been trying to pick up the pieces—I haven't even had a long-term goal. Who knows, maybe I can hire a private investigator to determine who sabotaged my restaurant dream."

At once, Lola's heart sank, and she felt awful for poor Levi. He was rudderless, his dream having crashed upon the rocks, leaving him to drift in the water. It almost made her want to let him have the money. Although she figured he'd win anyhow, as he was by far the better chef.

"Stayed tuned, everyone, till next week when you can see the next winner of *Shop till you Drop!*"

"Okay, you two. We'll see you back here at 6:30 a.m. sharp. Bring your A game," Marty said. "And you, Orchid, make sure you drink plenty of water." He gave her a wink and she smiled. Whatever. She had far more on her mind than being forever taunted for passing out on television.

Chapter Thirteen

LEVI couldn't believe he was in Los Angeles for the night, and instead of going out on the town, trying a new restaurant, or even taking a long walk, he remained in his hotel room pouting. If he at least knew where Lola was staying or what her phone number was, that would help. Something. Anything. He had tomorrow and then that was it. He hadn't even had a chance to plead his case. Although he was at least able to lobby on behalf of certain skills he'd mastered, how far would that take him?

He was bored after an hour so threw on shorts and a T-shirt and went for a run. Maybe he would sweat his angst out. Otherwise he'd fret the night away. God, he was so damn horny too. He couldn't believe he'd broken down that impenetrable wall surrounding Lola. Not that she didn't have good reasons for having constructed it. And he knew how lucky he was to have made it past the moat at least. So, sure, he'd managed to swim past crocodiles lurking in the waters, but still, that damned castle door was shut tight. Oh, what he would do to use his hard cock to ram that castle drawbridge open. He had a taste of what that would be like, quite literally, and he could still remember the feeling of his fingers sliding inside her warmth. It was something he was newly addicted to. Now he needed to figure out a way to convince Lola to give him another chance.

Upon his return to the hotel, he ran past Lola who was

on her way to the elevator.

"Hey there," he said, slowing to match her pace. "Going anywhere?"

"Oh. Hey." She pulled her key card from her pocket. "Nope. Took a little walk. Going back to my room for some room service and early bedtime."

"That's what I had planned as well. Care to join me for either or?" He grinned.

"I'm not sure that your definition of going to bed early and mine match right now."

"It can be left to interpretation."

"I'm not sure that's such a great idea."

"Why not? Well, let's at least have dinner together. I mean, you need to eat something. I need to eat something. It's healthy to share the communality of dining with others. Much better than eating alone watching Netflix."

Lola scrunched her nose as she pressed the elevator button. "Oh, I'm not sure…"

"Well, if one of us is sure, then that should tip it in the direction of certainty, right? Nature abhors a vacuum, and lack of commitment leads to a vacuum."

"You're spewing all sorts of bullshit tonight, aren't you?"

The elevator door opened and they stepped in. When it closed, he moved right up next to her.

"Anything to finish what we started earlier, Lol," he said, pulling her toward him so his body was pressed against hers, then drawing his tongue across her ear, eliciting a moan from her lips.

"You're not playing fair, Levi," she said yet pressed her hips toward his.

"All's fair in love and war."

She lifted a brow. "And which is ours?"

He continued to lick the shell of her ear and trailed his tongue along her jaw, to her chin, and down her throat. Pulling the thin strap of her camisole top down, he exposed her breast.

"Ahhh, God…" He fastened his mouth over her breast as she leaned back against the elevator's mirrored wall.

"More," she said, her voice breathy with desperation.

"Did you ever stop to think that security cameras are watching us?"

"I always wanted to be in pictures." She laughed.

"Does that turn you on to think people are watching me suck on your nipples?" He reached down her shorts and slipped his hand beneath the elastic edge of her panties, his fingers gliding with ease into the slick juices that had already started to flow.

"Yes. No. Maybe." She shook her head. He kind of loved that she didn't know how to answer that question. He'd be more than happy to drop trou right here and now and lift her up onto his hard cock, watching her pussy swallow him up in the mirrored walls.

"Should we give them an even better show?"

While it was a huge turn-on to think they could get caught, he also didn't want to risk another opportunity for someone to disrupt them at an important juncture.

The elevator dinged, and he fixed her top and pulled his hand from her pants right away. A couple entered the elevator and Levi knew they could smell her arousal. He pulled Lola closer and leaned over and suckled her neck gently.

"I want you to want me, Lola," he said, his fingers clasping hers as they watched the elevator pass floor after floor. Finally, the couple got out. "If I don't feel your warm pussy around my cock, I might just die."

Hard to Get

At long last, the elevator arrived at her floor. They were both panting when the doors opened. She stepped out and extended her hand to him, and he followed silently.

"I might be an incredible fool, but I want you. I've always wanted you, Levi."

With that, he grabbed her hand and pulled her in the direction they were heading. "I don't even know which one is your room."

She pulled him to a stop several doors down. He pressed her up against the door and kissed her hard, his tongue searching for hers, searching for approval, searching for the chance to make up for lost time.

"Give me the key or I'm going to take you right here."

She giggled as she slid it into the door and opened it. Then he lifted her and carried her to the bed, dropping her down in front of him. Quickly, he pulled her top over her head; she reached for the waistband of his shorts and shifted them down his hips while he removed his T-shirt and toed off his shoes and socks. He stood before her naked and desperate, and it was clear she knew it because she teased him, moving her hands everywhere but where he needed them to be. Finally, finally, she wrapped her fist around him and drew his cock into her warm mouth, sucking him hard, taking him deep, coaxing him so close to climax as he thrust his hips toward her lips.

"Fuck, Lola, I need to take you." He pulled back from her warm, wet mouth and scooted her up the bed so they could lie on their sides, face-to-face, their bodies pressed together. "God, I can't tell you how amazing it is to feel your warmth on my skin."

He reached for her leg and lifted it over his hip, spreading her open for him, and he pressed his hips forward till the swollen head of his cock was notched at the entrance to her body. She moaned loudly as he pressed into her slippery depths, the smooth glide of her juices welcoming him into her body. When he was seated as deep as he could go, he let out his breath and enjoyed the magical sensation of being so perfectly joined with her.

Lola was antsy, though. She ground herself up against him, silently telling him to do what he had to do, what she needed him to do, and so he began the slow slide out and back in, picking up the pace as she wrapped her leg tighter around his hip. He leaned forward and took her nipple into his mouth as she twirled his hair in her fingers with one hand and clutched his ass with the other.

"Ahhh, baby, I want you to come with me, Lol. I'm so close. Can you feel my cock getting harder inside you?"

She panted hard as she thrust her hips toward him, grinding and rubbing her clit against his cock. "Oh, Levi, right there, keep doing that."

His groin tightened, his cock felt impossibly full, and his balls pulled up tight in his body. That's when he let go, pulsing wave after wave of come into Lola's welcoming warmth, as her body convulsed, and she released on a loud moan, biting into Levi's shoulder as she came.

Chapter Fourteen

WELL, this was certainly not the plan for this evening, Lola thought as she lay stark naked, curled around Levi like a vine around an oak tree. She was still in the "everything is murky" department where he was concerned. It wasn't the wisest of moves to have sex—phenomenal sex, the kind she hadn't had since, oh, ten years ago. After Levi, on the rare occasions she even bothered to hook up with a guy, that's all it was—a hookup. Scratching an itch. Beyond that, no man she'd encountered was worth the bother. Sure, some guys were perfectly nice, but they weren't plan-a-future-with types. They were more like "my toilet is leaking, any idea how to fix it?" types. Which didn't sound very charitable, did it?

But Levi, ack, Levi was in a league of his own. The Levi Patton league. He was sweet, thoughtful, and kind and sexy as hell, not to mention an amazing lover. So, how was it that he caved to her stupid mother?

Lola thought about that. She hadn't even shared the worst of the worst about her mother with him. He was enough of an escape that she wanted to enjoy being with him without thinking about her. Her mom had always been Lola's chief competition, which was weird. It seemed like her mom was trying to make up for her own childhood by stealing the best of Lola's. That type of behavior was all Lola knew. In no way could she have suspected her mom of sabotaging the one relationship that mattered to her. What sense would it make to discuss all this with Levi? It was what it was.

After Levi, who knows, maybe her mom thought it would somehow bond them together, but instead, Lola drifted away from her mother. When she died suddenly, Lola was kind of ambivalent about it. On the one hand, sure, it was her mom. You're supposed to feel a certain way about your parents, right? And you're supposed to grieve losing them. But losing her mom changed nothing for Lola. It merely relieved her from having to deal with her mother's stuff, which wasn't such a bad thing. The good news was her grandpa was there for her, always had been. He must've recognized that Lola needed what her mom failed to provide. And he did his best to be there, to show up at her dance recitals and volleyball games and music concerts and take pictures of her before the prom. Lola's mom would've gotten dressed up to attend the prom.

Maybe Lola and Levi couldn't have been together successfully with her mother lurking in the background. Maybe her mother needed to be gone for them to have their own lives, independent of her.

Or maybe Lola needed to stop mooning over a long-lost love who'd resurfaced and instead focus on her goal of winning the cooking contest and launching her food truck.

Levi rolled over and tucked her head beneath his chin, wrapping his arms tightly around her. It felt so right... like what had been missing from her life for so long.

"You know," he said as he twirled her hair around his finger, "I couldn't tell you the last time I felt so right." He laughed. "That sounds weird, doesn't it?"

"Maybe?"

"I mean, for a long time after everything happened, I was kind of lost. I didn't know where to place my focus, so

Hard to Get

I put it into working hard, going home, and getting to sleep. When I succeeded professionally, it felt good to have landed there, but it seemed a little hollow. It was kind of like, 'Okay, you did this. But so what?' Not the way you'd feel if you, say, won your Olympic race or something. Something you'd aspired to for a while, worked hard to get to, but then meh. I liken it to getting to the top of a roller coaster and when you plunge down, you feel like you could nod off and go to sleep."

Lola laughed. "Not gonna lie. That's kind of the way too much of my adult life has been so far. Just plugging along. The best feeling I get is helping others who are in a trough like I was. I know how much it means to them to have someone who cares for them. But still, it seems like there's been something missing—like I assembled a thousand-piece puzzle and a couple of pieces are lost and it's frustrating that I'll never get it the way it's meant to be."

Levi leaned down and kissed her nose. "Do you think what each of us was missing was the other? Like we're each other's missing puzzle pieces? Or does that seem too much like a Hallmark movie solution?"

She laughed. "Maybe so. I don't know." She paused. "So has there been anyone else in your life?" She was afraid of the answer, but she had to ask.

"You sure you want to know? I kind of remember you as having a jealous streak."

"I'm a big girl now. I can take it."

"Nah, not really." He poked her in the ribs and got her to giggle. "I had my share of one-night stands, but nothing that got past that. To be honest, in the restaurant business it's not too easy to conduct normal relationships. You're around the kitchen staff most of the time and the waitstaff and working crazy late hours. I never liked the idea of hooking up with people at work—too much drama for me. There was a sous chef at my restaurant who was determined to be with me but I didn't bite."

"Maybe she was the one who sabotaged you?"

"Maybe. But I'm starting to not even want to know." He rolled over on his back and pulled her on top of him. "I'm learning that there are much more interesting ways to occupy your time than to dwell on the negative."

She straddled his hips and dipped her head down to kiss him. "Such as?"

"Such as learning every square inch of your body because I've missed it for so freaking long," he said, swiping his tongue along her lips till she opened her mouth for him. He reached up and played with her nipples as she slowly gyrated against him.

"You know you're playing with fire, Ms. Quigley," he said in a growl.

"Not to worry. I know the perfect way to manage this sort of wildfire."

The big question was how to handle this wildfire if it burned out of control?

Chapter Fifteen

LOLA and Levi waited in the lobby for the van to pick them up the next morning as if they hadn't been literally connected to one another for the better half of the night. With the final shoot for the competition looming, Levi wrestled with the best way to handle things. Yes, there would be some element of vindication in winning a cooking show on national television. But it was, after all, a reality show, so it wouldn't change much. Unless they decided to invite him back to do more shows. Could be a steady gig and some money, which would help him dig out of debt.

He'd started to think about what he wanted. For a good, long while, he hadn't even known. Did he care about what people thought of him anymore? Those who believed he was sloppy enough to let a rodent tail fall into the bouillabaisse he was serving weren't people he cared about. Those who knew him knew it was a set-up. And as far as who did it, he had his suspicions. But he was losing his taste for seeking justice. Life was too short to bother.

He'd considered throwing this competition to Lola so she could win and have her day in the sun. But if she found out, she'd flip her shit on him—he knew that all too well. She wanted to win this fair and square, so it had to be that way. If he did win, would she be bitter? He didn't want that either.

Oh, hell. Maybe he was being a little cocky. Maybe she

had what it took to whoop his ass anyhow. And if she did, he'd be nothing but proud of her.

They didn't speak on the bus ride over and they both entered the studio as if they were two separate entities, not rediscovered lovers who right now probably wanted nothing more than to drop everything and have wild monkey sex on the cashier's conveyor belt. The audience would love that, though the censors, not so much.

Marty greeted them both with a hearty handshake.

"Orchid! I trust you got a good night's sleep, you've had plenty of water, and you're ready to go?"

She threw a surreptitious glance at Levi. Depended on how you defined a good night's sleep.

"Okay, you two. Here's the game: dealer's choice. This time we pick your two main ingredients." He turned to Lola. "Lola, you get corn smut and canned prickly pears."

Lola's smile curved up on one side. She must've had something in mind already.

"And Levi, we know you're a man of good humor, so we're only giving you one ingredient to prepare however you see fit. I'll warn you, in case you still flinch at the mention of a tail, but it's oxtail."

They played one of those game show sound effects that sounded like "womp, womp" and Levi chose to laugh it off.

"You could've given me lobster tails, you know." Which generated a good laugh from the cast and crew.

"You both have one hour before time is up. On your mark, get set, go." He waved the black checkered flag and they were off.

Talk about a disadvantage. Oxtails were something that had to be cooked low and slow. Levi's one chance was to pan sear them, then use the Instant Pot and hope for the best. He planned to make the Roman dish coda alla vaccinara, a tomato-based oxtail stew. His first stop was the produce section, where he snapped up some fresh marjoram, a carrot, an onion, and celery. He moved on to the spice aisle for ground cloves and cinnamon. Next, he got a jar of tomato paste, a can of San Marzano peeled tomatoes, and a bottle of white wine. He then collected the flours and eggs he'd need to make a batch of pappardelle. Last, he visited the meat section for a chunk of pancetta before racing back to his station.

Luckily the oxtails were segmented already, so that saved him time. He drizzled olive oil in a large sauté pan and tossed the oxtails in, then chopped the fresh vegetables and pancetta in a rush, tossing them in with the oxtails. Man, he was speeding up the process to a dangerous degree on this, but he had no choice. Time was not on his side. As soon as the meat, veggies, and pancetta had browned enough, he tossed them into the Instant Pot, adding the tomato paste, wine, herbs, and canned tomatoes, squishing them between his fingers as he dropped them in. He set the Instant Pot and hoped for the best.

Next he started the pasta—mixing the flours, cracking his eggs into the center, blending with a fork, then kneading it. There was no time for chilling the dough, and since he was rolling out his pasta peasant-style, he didn't have to fear warm dough gumming up the pasta machine.

He made a ball and grabbed a rolling pin and rolled out the dough, then cut wide ribbons of pasta, setting them aside in little nested piles till he was ready to cook them. Glancing up at the clock, he saw there were five minutes left. He looked over at Lola and wondered what on earth she was doing with huitlacoche and how she knew what to do with it. She was something else, looking calm and collected as she prepped avocado slices for garnish.

He almost lost track of time, he was so engrossed in watching her, but luckily, he dropped the pasta in with time to spare. The Instant Pot indicated it was done, and he pulled out the oxtail stew, serving each helping atop the pappardelle and carefully wiping each plate before Marty called time.

As the judges clapped for the two remaining contestants, Levi and Lola looked at each other with relief in their eyes, and he extended his arms to give her a hug. Not like anyone would expect this meant anything more than friendly rivals making nice at the end of a tough battle.

"Judges are going to try Levi's first," Marty said. "Levi, any words of advice?"

"Yeah, be careful of any floating tails." He gave a wink and they all laughed. "But seriously, this is one of my favorite Roman dishes. The Roman butchers were called *vaccinari*, or cow workers, and the *vaccinara*, the butchers' wives, were skilled at taking bad cuts of meat and working their wonders on them. This is a dish many Romans savor. *Buon appetito*." He kissed his fingertips.

The first female judge took a bite and smiled. "The sauce is delectable. I love the pulpy slurry the celery has reduced down to. The pappardelle is maybe a tad bit undercooked. But overall, an ambitious undertaking."

The male judge was unhappy the oxtails weren't more tender. "If you'd had more time, maybe."

Levi wanted to say, "No shit, sherlock. But if you give me a meat that usually has to cook for three hours, what do you want, miracles?" But instead, he smiled and thanked the judge.

The last judge finally spoke. "I was hoping against hope for Chinese braised oxtails," she said. "Something my mother made when I was a child. My comfort food. I like what you've done with this and I give you credit for aiming high. We placed high expectations on you to make it happen, and you did a darned good job of it."

"Orchid, you're up next." Lola gave him two thumbs up. "Tell us what you've fixed."

"I'm grateful that you all chose to give me ingredients you knew I could handle," she said. "Since corn smut and prickly pear soup was my demo recipe when I applied to the show, it almost felt like an unfair advantage. But I'll take what I can when up against a pro." She nodded toward Levi. "So, now you all get to taste my take on chicken and huitlacoche soup with prickly pears."

The last judge commented first this time. "To be honest, I've been dying to try this soup ever since I saw it in your audition tape. Corn smut and prickly pear? Who would think to put those two ingredients together? And yet it's this crazy delicious sweet and savory combination, like eating dessert and dinner in one spoonful. I love it."

Judge number two said he would have preferred a homemade chicken stock. As if she'd had time to make that.

And the other judge gave it a ringing endorsement. "I'd love the recipe!" she said with a wink as she licked the spoon clean. Levi could see Lola beaming. He was too, on her behalf.

"Okay, judges. Time to make that final decision."

Lola and Levi stood side by side. He reached his hand out discreetly and clasped hers with his. "Good luck, Lola Bear," he whispered.

Chapter Sixteen

"WHICH chef is the winner of the hundred-thousand-dollar prize, judges?"

Lola was so anxious, she thought she might throw up. The three judges placed their hands on the hand of the domed plate cover and pulled it back, revealing Lola's dish. In an instant, confetti rained down from the ceiling, blinding amounts of it, sticking to their hair and their faces and their mouths. The judges left their seats to come extend congratulations, along with Marty.

"Does that mean I won? Or I lost?" Lola looked to Levi, her brows lifted in question.

"Lola, sweetie, you won!"

"I won?"

"Yes! You won!"

"Whoa. That's crazy. But I kinda feel woo—" and she never got to say "zy" before she headed for the floor. This time Levi was there to catch her before she hit hard.

"Oh, Lola, baby." He pulled her toward him while calling for someone to bring smelling salts. "Remind me never to spring any big surprises on you. It's clear you can't take the pressure."

He gently tapped on her cheeks to try to wake her. As soon as the nurse on duty opened the smelling salts she woke up, blinking her eyes. "What the heck happened?"

"Lola—you won! You're going to get to launch your

food truck!"

"But what about you—what about your comeback?"

"Sweetie, we can talk about that stuff later, but to be honest, the one thing that matters to me right now is you. The best comeback I could have ever hoped for was with you, and that's what this show has given me. Now let's get you up—you've got a check to receive."

Levi helped lift Lola to a standing position and stood behind her to be safe.

"Orchid, you are a delicate flower. We'll have to give you a year's supply of bottled water or something to keep you hydrated. But in the meantime, let me present this check for one hundred thousand dollars. We here at *Shop till you Drop* would like to also make a donation of food supplies for the truck once you're up and running because we believe in your mission. It's been a pleasure having you on the show and we wish you luck in your new business venture!"

Lola basked in the victory for a little while until it was time to go. Levi offered to get them an Uber back to the hotel.

In the Uber, he offered up lunch. "I've got some oxtail stew you might like."

She laughed. "You show me yours and I'll show you my corn smut."

He leaned over to kiss her. "Can I tell you how turned on I was with you working with smut?"

"You mean to tell me that corn fungus gets you hot and bothered? Sheesh! What doesn't turn you on?"

"Well, when you put it like that, it loses some of its charm."

They laughed.

"I don't know about you, but I could use a shower after all that cooking," Levi said once they were back in her room.

"I could be persuaded."

"Oh yeah? What would it take?"

"Maybe if you can help me get this off." She reached for her sweaty tank, which was splattered with corn smut. He lifted it from the hem, up and over her head. "And how about this too?" She pointed at her bra, which she'd already unclipped.

"If you insist." Inch by inch, he slid the straps from her shoulders, standing to admire her breasts. "You know, we could bypass the shower altogether and I could lick you clean." His eyes twinkled.

"Oh no, I'm enjoying the process, thanks."

He nodded. "Gotcha. So what's next?"

"These." She pointed down to her jeans. "They're so tight. Maybe you could slip them off?"

"It would be my pleasure." He unbuttoned the top and slid the zipper down, then shifted them off her hips, along her legs, and down to the floor, where she stepped out of them.

"Is there anything else you need help with?"

She held her arms up over her head, which lifted her breasts. His eyes followed her every move. She twirled around once. "It's only that these are still on, and I can't shower with panties on."

"In that case, allow me," he said as he slipped them off, easing a finger between her legs while he did it. "Maybe this might help."

"More, please."

He licked two fingers and put them back between her legs, slicking them along her already-wet pussy lips. "How does that feel?"

"Ohhh, sooo, good," she said. "And while you're at it, could you please maybe suck here?" She placed her hand beneath a breast, offering it up to his waiting mouth.

"I thought you'd never ask." Gently, he licked around the areola on one breast and sucked hard, taking little nips with his teeth. With each gentle bite, she moaned loudly. "Oh, you like that, do you?"

She nodded.

"You want more?"

"So much more."

"Like what?"

Lola kind of liked this dirty talk. She wasn't used to saying out loud what she wanted to have done to her or what she wanted to do to a man. But she was feeling emboldened.

"I want to sit on your face while you lick me till I come," she said, fighting the need to blush.

"That could be arranged, you little horny girl. But first—" He reached for her as he pulled off his shirt and stripped down his pants. He lay down on the bed. "Now come here."

She walked to the bed and reached down to clasp his hard cock. "Uh-uh. Not yet." He wagged his finger at her. "You, come here. I want you facing the headboard as you straddle my mouth. And then you're gonna pretend you're riding a horse."

She followed his instructions and held on to the headboard while she lowered herself to his mouth. As she thrust herself against his tongue, it was the most incredible sensation. She could control the tempo and the pressure and the speed of her arousal with each stroke of his tongue.

He hummed as she pressed against his face, and the vibration ratcheted up her arousal even more.

"Oh, fuck, Levi, this is amazing." She was overcome with the sensations. Her pelvic floor tightened and the convulsions of her climax spread throughout her body, fireworks igniting everywhere, as she flooded his mouth with her juices.

Levi wasted no time shifting positions so that he had her on all fours, and he entered her from behind, grasping her hips as he thrust deep inside her. He reached around and played with her clit. In a million years, Lola didn't think she could come again, but within minutes, she felt the sensation climbing as he pressed in deep, releasing waves of come inside her warm pussy. They collapsed in a heap on the bed.

"So much for that shower, eh?" she said.

"No bones left to even stand. Next time." Levi tucked her beneath his arm as they both drifted off to the deepest sleep they'd had in ages.

Lola lay in bed staring at Levi who snored quietly next to her. She couldn't believe the turn of events over the past seventy-two hours and how much her life had changed so suddenly. It all felt so incredible. But there was one thing she felt could make it truly complete.

Levi startled awake and looked up at her staring at him.

"Everything okay, Lol?"

"Couldn't be better." She smiled. "Although, I was thinking one thing might make it even better."

"Oh, yeah? And what could that be?"

"I was thinking how nice it would be to have a partner in this new undertaking. Someone who knows his way around a kitchen. Someone who knows how to run a business. Someone who gives amazing head."

He blurted out a laugh. "Did you have someone in mind? Like maybe the UPS guy?"

"I was thinking more along the lines of someone who looks dapper in a white chef's jacket but also looks amazing with nothing on at all."

"You aren't talking about Andre, I hope?" They both laughed.

"Nah, I'm not a beard gal." She leaned over him, playing with the hair on his chest in the early morning light. "What do you think?"

He lifted a brow. "You sure you don't want this to be your thing?"

"I'd like nothing better than for it to be *our* thing."

"Well, we do have to make up for a lot of lost time," he said. "And working together twenty-four seven will feel like we've been together twice as long."

"In that case, consider it a done deal. And I've been thinking, maybe in that case, we can call the truck 'Happily Ever After.'"

"I can't think of a better name for it."

"Or for the two owners who plan to live that way. Together. Happily ever after. Finally."

Thank you!

Thank you so much for reading *Hard to Get!* I hope you enjoyed it! If so, please help others find this book:

1. Help other people find this book by writing a review.

2. Sign up for my new releases email so you can find out about the next book as soon as it's available and get fun giveaways.
    http://eepurl.com/baaewn

3. Like my Facebook page.
    www.facebook.com/jennygardinerbooks

And I love to hear from readers! Let me know what you think about my books! You can write to me at jenny@jennygardiner.net, and visit me on the web at www.jennygardiner.net.

Read on for a teaser of the next book in the Hard to Get series – *Hard to Get Lucky*.

About *Hard to Get Lucky*:

Not such a cutie patootie...

Alyssa Heyward has held a powerful grudge against Josh "The Mad Tooter" Trumbull for the better part of her life. Not that obsessing over something that happened when you were a tween is a particularly helpful thing to do for your mental health. And not like she's dwelt on it forever. In fact, she hadn't considered it—or him—for a long, long time… Until he shows up at her door as the new general contractor set to do major renovations on her house. Which instantly resurrects all of those old feelings about the sleepover at her best friend's house when she ever-so-reluctantly agreed to partake in her first (and last) game of spin-the-bottle. When the creepiest boy in the Fourth grade spun, and the bottle pointed toward Alyssa, she thought her life was over indeed. And when she stood as far away from him in the dark storage closet instead of submitting to an unwanted kiss from the boy everyone knew had eaten a fly in the cafeteria and whose propensity for, um, breaking wind in all the wrong places (not to mention belching like a bullfrog) were the hallmark of his personality, she hoped she'd dodged a bullet. Until Josh Trumbull exited the closet and told everyone that instead of kissing him, Alyssa had emitted a noxious fume in the closed space.

Perhaps the high point of Josh Trumbull's prank-filled childhood happened at a spin-the-bottle party, when the girl he fostered a wicked crush on refused to grant him that one little kiss, and instead treated him like a pariah when they were sequestered in the dark confines of the kissing closet. Quick on his feet with a rejoinder, Josh popped out of the dark room and told all his buddies that Alyssa had pooted in there, killing all romantic notions of a first kiss.

He hadn't given this moment a second thought for the rest of his life. Until now. When he rings the doorbell of the woman whose home he's set to renovate and when she opens the door, her face falls, much like it did when that spinning bottle pointed straight at her nearly fifteen years earlier. Leaving him to wonder: does he have any chance of rebuilding a relationship with the woman who hates him most as he rebuilds her home?

Read on for a sneak peek.

Chapter One

15 years earlier

ALYSSA Heyward had been looking forward to Caitlyn Colby's birthday sleepover party for weeks. This would be the first party she'd been to since moving to town. She and Caitlyn had hit it off quite readily, so this would be a great chance to hang out with some of the other kids from Roland Clark Elementary School who she only usually saw in passing during classes. And there would be boys for the birthday party part—Alyssa's first boy party! She was nervous but excited.

On the day of the party, she'd pulled her long, blonde hair into a French braid—with help from her mom—and even snuck into her mom's make-up and applied a discreet amount of eye shadow to highlight her pale green eyes. She put on her favorite knit sundress with the rainbows on it over a pair of black capri leggings. She knew she'd fit right in.

At the party, things went great early on: all the kids got to swim in Caitlyn's backyard pool, Caitlyn's dad grilled the best hot dogs and hamburgers. The birthday cake was her favorite: yellow cake with buttercream frosting. All good. But then the kids migrated to Caitlyn's basement and someone decided they all had to play Spin-the-Bottle.

Alyssa wasn't particularly enlightened about boys and had certainly never kissed one. There were some cute boys in her classes and then there were some who grossed her out. Like that boy Josh Turnbull, who was super gross and whose claim to dubious fame was that he'd eaten a fly in the cafeteria, although perhaps even worse, he loved to burp and fart like he was some sort of pig in a farmyard. She'd been completely dismayed to see him at the party, and of course he behaved predictably. After he jammed a hot dog down his throat in record time, he'd mustered up the loudest, most disgusting burp imaginable, like some totally vomitrocious percussion instrument. He wouldn't be so awful if he was so awful if he hadn't been so continuously crass—he could almost be cute, with his kind brown eyes, and she kind of liked when boys had wavy dark hair. But yuck, there was no way she'd even stand near Josh Trumbull, even if someone paid her a million dollars.

After the twenty or so kids got down to the basement, they all played video games for a while in the room where the girls had already set up their sleeping bags. Alyssa watched from the corner of her eye to be sure stinky Josh, who kids called The Mad Tooter, didn't settle down near her bag. The last thing she wanted was him smelling up her comfy sleeping bag with the kitties and puppies on it.

Then some really tall boy named Luis stood up and let out a whistle to get everyone's attention as he pulled out a bottle of Coke he'd tucked into the waistband of his jeans.

"Gather 'round," he said, motioning to the crowd with his hands. "Everyone get in a big circle here. Now we're going to have some real fun."

Oh god, what was he talking about? Alyssa wished she could slip upstairs and maybe grab another slice of that delicious cake, or even maybe help Mrs. Colby with the dishes. She feared the telltale bottle could only be the harbinger of bad things to come.

He plunked the bottle down in the center of the group of kids who were tittering and giggling and whispering.

"All right, people," he said. How someone his age could have such command of a group mystified Alyssa. She was perfectly happy to blend into the room and not be noticed. "I'm gonna get this party started with the first spin of the bottle. If the bottle lands pointing at a boy, I get to spin again. But if it lands pointing to a girl, then we go there—" He aimed his thumb over his shoulder, pointing toward the storage closet where Alyssa knew for a fact Caitlyn's much older sister Samantha would to go smoke cigarettes and drink beer with her friends. Caitlyn and Alyssa had caught them on more than one occasion in there when Alyssa had slept over.

Alyssa's eyes widened. By "we go there" did he mean what she was afraid he meant? This was the dreaded game, the one all Fourth graders had heard about, the one that instilled fear into the hearts of burgeoning tweens everywhere. Where you're forced by peer pressure to slip off alone into a closet with someone you don't even know and press your lips together. Ugh. This terrified her.

Luis' bottle stopped, pointing toward a quiet girl named Ginny whose face turned bright red when she knew she was the first victim. She glanced around at her friends to see if they would grant her a respite, but instead her looks were met with jeers and cheers.

Luis extended his arm and his hand grabbed Ginny's and the next thing everybody knew, they were inside that closet and everyone in the circle waited in near silence till they'd done the deed.

Alyssa didn't know what to make of things when they came out and Luis was licking his lips—literally, like a wolf after finishing off a farmer's sheep. Ginny was still blushing, only she had a slight grin on her face, which was better than the flat-out tears Alyssa had half-expected.

Round after round happened with girls and boys pairing off for their slow-walk to the storage closet.

Then came Josh Trumbull's turn. Just to make sure his presence was known, he took a fat swig of his own bottle of soda and then forced out a belch that practically vibrated throughout the room. He was disgusting. He stood in the center of the group and bent down to spin the bottle, and – no lie—tooted out a blast of air from his backside that made Alyssa cringe. Pity the poor girl who would be stuck in there with him. She'd need a gas mask.

He gave the bottle a dramatic whirl with a strong flick of his wrist, and Alyssa stared as the bottle circled around before slowing. She clasped her fingers together in prayer. *"Pleasepleaseplease don't let it be me,"* repeated on an endless loop in her head.

The bottle seemed to enter into some time warp slow-mo as it finally crept to a dead stop pointing directly at Alyssa. The girls on either side of her even shifted away from her, to ensure there was no confusion as to who the victim would be.

Alyssa could actually feel her face fall. It felt as if the blood had drained from it. For a split second she wondered if she might just faint dead away, right then and there. Which would be equally mortifying. Talk about a lose-lose proposition. Although maybe passing out would be the hall pass she needed to get out of this dirty deed. Josh Turnbull stood in front of her, performing dire pelvic thrusts toward her, making her almost gag, as he crooked his pointer finger toward her, then curling it back toward him so she knew in no uncertain terms she had no choice but to suffer through this indignity.

She closed her eyes and tried to invoke happy thoughts: beach trips with her family, swimming in the ocean with her dog Lupe, snuggling at bedtime with her kitten Muffin, an A on her history test. She stood up and her bare feet practically betrayed her by obliging Josh Turnbull's coaxing finger. She followed a few paces behind him, hoping it was clear to all in this room that she had no choice but to subjugate herself for the greater good of her contemporaries from Roland Clark Elementary School. There was no hope of a stay of execution. She gulped hard: this was the twenty-first century version of walking the gangplank on a pirate ship on the Barbary Coast.

The light was on in the room when they entered it, giving Alyssa enough time to scour the horizon and see that her safest harbor was in the far left corner of the room, just past the stacked boxes marked "Christmas Decorations", but then Josh Turnbull turned to face his audience as he dramatically pulled the cord, extinguishing the light and bathing the room in darkness as he slammed the door for effect.

Alyssa wanted to cry. God, if she had to put her mouth near his, would it smell like dead flies? Probably not, because the other part of him that always stunk would overpower it. This was so unfair. Why couldn't it have been someone like Christian Masterson, who at least chewed gum 24/7 so would have fresh, minty breath? Or better yet Rodrigo Lopez, who everyone knew would only share his kisses with the boys. She'd be totally safe and kiss-free in the dark with him.

She stood stock-still, the lingering aroma of noxious cigarette smoke and stale beer permeating the air. The silence in the room was agonizing. She surely wasn't going to say a peep. Opening her mouth seemed a bad idea anyhow, what with his mouth lurking threateningly somewhere in close proximity.

"So, uh, you coming over any time soon?" he finally said.

"No, thank you," Alyssa said.

"*No thank you* as in you're not coming over here and you'd rather I come to you?"

She shook her head, not like he could see it. "No thank you, I'm fine here in this corner all alone."

"You're not even going to give me a kiss?"

"No thank you." She sounded like a broken record.

"That's lame."

They stood there, barely conversing, with Alyssa only repeating her new, albeit fairly polite, mantra.

"Fine, then. If you're gonna be that way about it."

Alyssa didn't know how someone could command bodily functions at whim like this boy could, but sure enough he could, and he discharged the stinkiest, loudest emission of bodily gas that she'd ever encountered in her short time on earth.

"That's disgusting," she said, plugging her nose with her fingers.

"Takes one to know one," he snarled. Which didn't even make sense, but whatever.

Enough arduous time had passed that people—actually, just the stupid boys—had started pounding on the door, so Josh Turnbull opened it wide, the brightness near-blinding after having been in complete darkness for several minutes.

Everyone clamored to find out how it went.

"Well," he said, standing in the middle of the circle as Alyssa slunk back to her spot and sat down. "We never got around to kissing because she let out a huge fart and stunk up the whole room."

"Ewwwww," all of the girls shouted.

"Cool," said one guy. Another guy gave her a thumbs up.

Everyone turned to look at Alyssa, who was hanging her head, mortified.

The rest of the night was a bit of a blur. Alyssa did her best to blend in with the background. People kept coming up to her and asking her if she'd really farted in there, and she was just so upset and disgusted that she could barely speak.

It was the last time she ever had anything to do with Josh Trumbull for the rest of her academic career, for which she couldn't have been more thrilled.

Chapter Two

ALYSSA was just finishing breakfast when the doorbell rang. Finally, the contractor must be here to get started on the long-awaited addition she was adding onto her house.

She'd been lucky and had some unexpected success in her writing career, when her first novel hit it big—something most writers hope their whole lives for. What that meant was some welcome financial security after years of toiling in obscurity. And it meant the tiny fixer-upper she'd purchased for super cheap just before she'd quit her job to write full-time was finally going to morph into the cozy home she'd envisioned. Aside from an overhaul of her dingy kitchen, she was adding on a whole new two-story section to the house, which would mean a guest bedroom for when friends visited, a gorgeous black-bottom swimming pool out back, but most importantly, a dedicated office/study where she could focus while writing, rather than hunkered down over the dining room table as she'd done for years now.

The housing boom meant that she'd lost three general contractors to bigger jobs just as they were about to undertake construction. The last one was a kind man, though, who'd felt badly enough about it that he promised he'd send someone reliable in his stead. And that someone was waiting for Alyssa to open the door.

She felt an inexplicable need to primp for a second before so doing, stupidly thinking if she looked decent enough and not like, say, a bleary-eyed, bedheaded, coffee-breathed writer who'd stayed up till almost dawn to work on her latest novel, the guy would stick around and actually do the work. She was tired of waiting.

She ran her fingers through her hair and slid her glasses up on her head as she pulled the door open.

"Hi!" She blurted out before having a chance to un-blurt it. Because standing before her was none other than Josh "The Mad Tooter" Turnbull—unmistakable in his appearance despite the passage of some fifteen years. She could instantly feel her face fall, the broad beam of a smile instantly transforming into a grimace that spoke volumes.

No greater humiliation than those foisted upon you in childhood linger quite as bitterly. At least that's what Alyssa told herself as she ground her molars together with such intensity she thought she'd crack a filling. And the shame cast upon her at the ripe age of was it ten? nine? clearly had lingered far more intensely than she would have imagined. Because the mere sight of that dirty ratfink Josh "the Mad Tooter" Trumbull instantly skyrocketed her back to that embarrassing night in Caitlyn Colby's basement.

She squinted her eyes into something that might easily be mistaken for a solid glare, but she hoped he'd see as the look of a woman who is thoroughly unfamiliar with him, thinking maybe she could pretend that she had no idea who he was. He clearly had to know who she was because the other contractor must have given him her name.

"Alyssa!" he said, reaching out his arms for a hug, of all the damned things, "So great to see you after all these years!"

A silence fell over them as he stood at the threshold to her home—good lord, the threshold to her life, since he was going to be in her home every damned day until he finished this huge project, while she tried to write and function and not simmer in rage.

This is what it's come to? In order to finally fix up her grungy, 1950's-era Northern Virginia red brick rambler –the only house she could afford with eye-popping DC-area prices when she bought it—was to welcome her lifelong nemesis into said home, and pretend she was happy with him being there?

She closed her eyes and mentally counted to ten. She opened them and then fixed the grimace so that her mouth was merely a tight line across her face.

"Josh? Josh 'The Mad Tooter' Trumbull? Well, who'd have thought I'd ever be seeing you ever again?"

Worse still, who'd have thought she'd have to practically share her life with him for the next several months? At least this time she wasn't going to be expected to kiss him.

Hard to Get Lucky – February 2021

About Jenny

Jenny Gardiner is an award-winning #1 Kindle bestselling author who has published 37 novels, a memoir, and a collection of essays. Her work has been found in Ladies Home Journal, the Washington Post, Marie-Claire.com, Paste Magazine, and on National Public Radio. She is an occasional essayist on regional NPR affiliate WVTF-FM, and wrote a humorous column in Charlottesville's Daily Progress for over a decade as well as a food column for Cville Weekly Magazine. She has worked as a publicist for a United States senator, and as a freelance photographer, photographing such notable public figures as Prince Charles, Elizabeth Taylor, and the President of Uganda. She's been the volunteer coordinator for the Virginia Film Festival for ten years. She's really bad at math.

Find her at www.jennygardiner.net